An Unexpected Amish Romance

Stephanie Swift

Published by Trellis Publishing, 2021.

AN UNEXPECTED AMISH ROMANCE

First edition. July 3, 2021.

ISBN: 979-8224666386

Written by Stephanie Swift.

AN UNEXPECTED AMISH ROMANCE

STEPHANIE SWIFT

Andrea Miles sat on a blanket beside her aunt Theresa and took a sip of her lemonade as they watched the activities unfold from their quiet little corner of the field. To say it was interesting seeing grown men hopping around in burlap sacks would be an understatement. When two of the men bumped into each other during the race and went tumbling to the ground, she covered her mouth and stifled a laugh.

"You would think they were children the way they act sometimes," her aunt remarked with a giggle. "They look forward to these games every year."

It wasn't often she was able to attend her aunt Theresa and uncle Luke's annual homecoming service in the small Amish community, so she enjoyed the festivities while they lasted. When she visited the first time, almost five years prior, she worried the congregation would snub her, since her father, who once belonged to the fold, never returned during his Rumspringa when he was sixteen years old.

She'd heard stories of their way of life since she was a youngster, but it wasn't something her father talked about often. A few days after her 21st birthday, she decided to throw caution to the wind and travel to Lancaster to meet her relatives, even though her father disapproved at first. Since then, she'd visited many times, and she always tried to make it to homecoming.

"I wish Raymond was here to see this," her aunt commented. "I bet he would be right in the middle of it."

She smiled when she said it, but it was such a rare occasion for her to mention her father's name, Andrea wasn't sure how to respond. They never discussed what happened during that Rumspringa, when Theresa decided to return home afterwards while Andrea's father went his own way in the world.

"Head's up!"

Fortunately, she didn't have to come up with a reply as a loud male voice interrupted the stillness and made them both jump. Andrea caught sight of a volleyball as it fell from the sky and landed a few feet away from them before a man she didn't recognize picked it up and jogged toward them.

"I'm sorry about that," he said. "I really need to help these kids work on their serve."

The corners of his mouth curved upward into a grin, and Andrea groaned as she felt her cheeks flush. He was quite handsome, with dark brown hair and the lightest green eyes she'd ever seen. He was also tall, and when he stopped in front of her, his broad shoulders nearly blocked the sun from her view.

Andrea and Theresa both stood at the same time, and when her aunt took Andrea's cup of lemonade from her hand, she gave her a curious look.

"I believe it's time for a refill," her aunt said.

Andrea didn't miss her sly smile and wink as she turned and headed for the refreshment table, and she was so embarrassed she felt like crawling under a rock.

"I don't believe we've met before. I'm Jonathan Henning."

He held out a hand and Andrea tentatively shook it. His skin was callused and warm, and the sensation made her shiver from her head straight to her toes.

"Andrea Miles," she replied, shyly. "It's nice meeting you."

His eyes swept over her attire and Andrea looked down at her floral dress and heels. It definitely wasn't the Amish clothing he was probably used to seeing, but it was the most decent and flattering dress she could find in her closet that would draw the least attention.

"No, I'm not from around here, but may have already guessed that by now. I'm visiting my aunt Theresa and uncle Luke. I live a couple of hours north in Laurel Springs."

He nodded as he tucked the volleyball underneath his arm.

"I haven't lived here long, so I'm still trying to get to know everyone. I moved from Ohio about eight months ago to care for my niece and nephew after my brother and sister-in-law passed away."

Andrea's hand flew to her chest. "Oh no...I'm so sorry."

He gave her a wistful smile before turning his attention to the center of the field where several young children were gathered around a volleyball net. "Thank you. The little one with red hair is my nephew, Ben. He's five years old. My niece, Rachel, is the one in the green dress and strawberry blonde hair. She's seven years old. They keep me on my toes all the time."

Andrea grinned. She could easily tell them apart from the crowd just by their unique hair color, and they were so adorable she couldn't help but smile.

"I'm a school nurse, so I've seen my share of precocious kids, but they don't look like a handful at all."

He threw his head back and laughed, and the deep, masculine sound sent another rush of liquid heat coursing through her veins.

"Don't let those sweet faces fool you," he whispered. "Ben! Rachel!"

The two children looked his way, and when he motioned for them to come join them, Rachel took off sprinting in their direction, but Ben lagged several feet behind.

His niece was quick to introduce herself before Jonathan had the chance to, and Andrea noticed right away her eye color closely resembled the same haunting shade of green as her uncle's. Even at just seven years old, she was quite stunning and had the flawless complexion of a porcelain doll.

Unlike Rachel, when Ben finally made it to Jonathan's side, he didn't say a word, and Andrea could tell he didn't have the same sunny disposition as his sister. Jonathan placed a hand on his shoulder and attempted to coax him into talking.

"Ben, this is Miss Andrea Miles," he announced. "Wait...is it Miss or Mrs.?"

Andrea blushed again. "It's Miss."

Ben didn't budge, and Andrea tried to help things along by giving him a big smile and holding out her hand for him to shake. In her line of work, she was used to children being shy when they first met her, so she knelt down in front of him so they were eye-to-eye.

"Hello Ben. It's very nice meeting you."

He was hesitant at first, but he finally reached out his little hand and put it in hers. Andrea frowned when she noticed how hot his hand was, and when she eyed him more closely, she could tell that something wasn't right. His cheeks were red and his gaze was glassy and distant, as if he was looking right through her.

She gave Jonathan a concerned look. "Has he been sick recently?"

Jonathan shook his head. "Not that I know of. Why?"

Andrea stood, but she didn't take her eyes off Ben, who immediately began to cower behind Jonathan's legs.

"I'm just curious. His feels like he may have a little fever."

Jonathan furrowed a brow as he looked down at Ben and tried to lure him out of hiding. At that time, Bishop Matthews got everyone's attention by letting out a loud whistle and inviting them all inside the church for the afternoon service, which would conclude the day's homecoming activities.

"I'll keep a close eye on him," Jonathan said, as the four of them began making their way to the church. "I remember my brother saying one time that Ben used to have a terrible time with allergies, so that may be what's wrong."

She tried to smile and appear more positive than she felt. Even though she'd just met Ben, she was almost certain it wasn't allergies because his symptoms said otherwise. Still, he wasn't her patient, and Jonathan didn't ask for her advice, so she remained quiet and made a mental note to check on him the next day.

* * * *

Jonathan glanced at the clock on the wall for what felt like the millionth time. It was nearing midnight, and the house was eerily quiet, except for the raspy sound of Ben's breathing as he slept in the tiny twin bed beside him. For two hours he'd sat in his rocking chair and watched as Ben's chest rose and fell with each haggard breath – hoping and praying that his fever would break.

Jonathan wiped the sweat from his brow and rested his head against the back of the chair. He wasn't used to this – would never get used to it. Before his brother and sister-in-law died, he'd never even contemplated having children, and he'd never dreamed of taking care of someone else's. Why they chose to appoint him as legal guardian over Ben and Rachel was anyone's guess because he didn't have a clue. He could barely take care of the farm and animals they also left him in charge of.

Ben's moaning stirred him from his reverie, and as he leaned over and placed a hand against his forehead, his heart fell to his feet. It seemed as if no amount of pacing the floors, hoping, or praying would make his fever go away. If anything, his little body felt even warmer than before.

"Uncle Jonathan, is Ben going to be okay?"

Jonathan looked over his shoulder and caught Rachel standing in the open doorway, rubbing her eyes with her fists. As she walked over to join him, he noticed right away the hesitation in her demeanor as she glanced back and forth between him and Ben. He wanted to put her at ease, but he didn't know what to say or what to do.

He sighed. If only children came with instruction manuals.

"*Yah*," he replied. "He's just resting."

That seemed to satisfy her as her face softened and she sat down on the bed beside her brother. They sat in silence for a long while until Ben moaned again and opened his eyes. He looked terrified as he attempted to sit up, and when he started crying, it felt as if someone reached inside Jonathan's chest and gripped him...*hard*.

Jonathan tried to keep him calm, but Ben wouldn't have it. As he flailed his arms and tried to get up, Rachel jumped off the bed and took several frightened steps away from them.

"Let me go!" Ben yelled. "Leave me alone!"

Jonathan's heart raced as he wrapped his arms around Ben's body to keep him from hurting himself, and after several tense minutes, he felt him go limp in his arms, but his crying only intensified. He didn't know much, but he did know that Ben's hysteria was more than likely caused by his fever, and that scared him.

"Rachel, I need you to put on your shoes and coat, okay? We've got to get Ben to a doctor."

Without another word, she raced from the room, and as Jonathan wrapped Ben in a warm blanket to shield him from the cool night air, he silently prayed for God to give him the wisdom and strength to get Ben the help he needed. He didn't know what to do or where to turn. He could put him in the carriage and take Ben to the hospital in Lancaster, but that would take too long.

An image of Andrea flitted across his mind and stopped him in his tracks. *Yes!* Andrea was a nurse, and she was visiting the Hammonds family, who lived only a couple of houses down the road from him. If he could get to her, she could drive them to the hospital in her car or use her cellphone to call for an ambulance. Maybe it was the adrenaline, or perhaps just divine intervention, but it felt like the right thing to do, and he wasted no time in getting Ben and Rachel to the carriage.

The seconds passed by in slow motion, and as Jonathan lifted Ben inside, he did his best to remain as calm and steady as possible, so he wouldn't send Rachel into a panic.

"Do you mind letting Ben rest his head on your lap while I drive?"

She nodded in agreement as he laid Ben on the seat and rested his head on her legs. He was deathly still, and his face was pale as a ghost, but he smiled at Rachel to keep her from worrying, despite the fear that held him firmly in its grasp.

Rachel kept the blanket securely tucked around his body, and as Jonathan crawled into the driver's seat and grabbed the reins, he considered what a great big sister she was, despite the obvious worry that darkened her sweet face.

Jonathan steered the horse and carriage out of the barn and onto the main dirt road. As he turned right, he looked into the distance where the Hammonds house was located, and he breathed a sigh of relief when he saw the glow of a lantern streaming from one of the windows. Although it took only a couple of minutes to reach the Hammonds driveway, the time seemed to pass by very slowly.

Jonathan pulled up on the reins and jumped from the carriage before it came to a full stop. Ben opened his eyes briefly and cried out when he took him in his arms and slowly descended the steps, with Rachel trailing closely behind. He walked hurriedly toward the front porch, and as he climbed the steps, someone opened the front door.

Andrea.

"Oh my God...what's wrong?" she asked.

She stepped aside to let them enter the den, where he carried Ben to the sofa.

"He needs help," Jonathan remarked. "His fever won't go down, and he keeps drifting in and out of consciousness."

The Hammonds walked in the room at that time, and as soon as Mrs. Hammonds saw Ben's sweat-soaked hair, she went to the kitchen to retrieve a cool wet dishrag, which she placed against his temple.

"I'm changing clothes and driving you to the emergency room," Andrea stated, resolutely.

Jonathan didn't argue, and as she ran from the room he turned his attention back to Ben. Rachel sat down at her brother's feet and began humming softly as she rubbed his legs. The sweet gesture brought tears to his eyes.

"Mrs. Hammonds, I hate to impose, but would you mind if Rachel..."

She held up a hand and stopped him mid-sentence. "You don't have to ask. Of course, she can stay with us."

Andrea reappeared moments later, and his breath caught and held when he noticed she'd changed from her gown and robe into a pair of jeans and a long-sleeved shirt. Her light brown hair cascaded in waves over her shoulders as she rushed around, gathering her car keys and purse, and he was momentarily distracted by her beauty.

Jonathan shook his head fervently to clear his mind. *Stop it, Jonathan. You're from two different worlds. Don't even go there.*

"Okay, I'm ready," she announced. "Let's go."

Without another word, Jonathan lifted Ben in his arms and followed Andrea to her car while Rachel and the Hammonds watched from the doorway. When Andrea opened the back door, he carefully slid inside and settled Ben comfortably on his lap while she took her place in the front seat behind the steering wheel.

She glanced at him from the rearview mirror before starting the car, and he could see the worry etched across her beautiful face. Ben stirred in his arms and moaned, and as he pulled him close, he silently prayed that God would take control and heal his little body.

If this was what being a parent felt like, he couldn't help but wonder if he would make it to the other side unscathed. Would his brother and sister-in-law be proud of how he was taking care of their children?

Jonathan frowned. Somehow...he doubted it.

* * * *

Andrea returned to the hospital waiting room with two steaming cups of coffee and found Jonathan standing at the window, staring blankly into the distance. The room was empty except for one elderly gentleman who had spent most of his time dozing in a chair since their arrival. As Andrea tiptoed to Jonathan's side, she took a deep breath and smiled big, in the hopes that her positive demeanor would rub off on him.

He'd barely uttered two words since their arrival, and even though Ben was doing better and resting comfortably in the emergency room, you would think the news was dire by the tortured look on his face. Andrea leaned against the window sill and handed him one of the cups, which he took without so much as a glimpse in her direction.

She sighed.

"I just saw Dr. Sloan in the corridor on my way to the vending machine, and he said Ben's still asleep, and his vitals are stable. It shouldn't be long before you can go see him," she said.

He took a sip of his coffee and nodded. His gaze was focused on the people walking along the sidewalk outside the hospital, and Andrea tried not to get impatient while waiting for him to say something – *anything*. She knew he was worried, and she understood that. It certainly wasn't the first time she'd had to comfort the stressed-out parent of a sick child, and it wouldn't be the last.

"It seems like every time I turn around, I'm failing them in some way."

He said it so softly she almost missed it, but her heart did a tiny flip-flop inside her chest when he finally spoke.

"My brother and sister-in-law would be so disappointed if they could see us right now," he continued.

Andrea swallowed hard and silently prayed for wisdom and the right words to ease his mind. She knew very little about their home life, but she could tell by the look on his face that their history together hadn't been smooth sailing.

"Jonathan, my father was Amish, so I know that most people in the faith don't agree with traditional medicine, but if the flu isn't treated right away, it can develop into pneumonia. If we hadn't brought Ben to the hospital..."

He held up a hand to stop her.

"It's not that," he replied. "Nothing would've kept me from getting Ben the help he needed. It doesn't matter to me how the people in my community might feel about it. He's my responsibility – not theirs."

Her heart did another somersault when his handsome face contorted into a serious expression and she detected the determination in his voice. If she didn't know the situation, she would've never guessed he was Ben's uncle and not his father because the fierce love he felt for him was plainly evident in his reaction.

"I was two years older than him, but Tom, my brother, was always the mature one when we were growing up. He kept me out of trouble *so* many times, but her never ratted me out to our parents...even though he probably should have because I definitely deserved it."

His gaze took on another faraway look as Andrea rested her head against the cool glass and watched him while he talked. His face and posture softened as he reminisced, and she waited silently for him to continue. When he was calm and reserved, his deep voice was a soothing reprieve, especially after such a chaotic evening.

"I can still picture the stern look on his face when he used to break up the many fights I got into at school. He would say, 'Jonathan Douglas Henning, God doesn't like ugly', and he would proceed to recite every scripture he could think of from Genesis to Revelations to try and save my soul."

They both laughed, and she could almost picture a younger version of him, picking fights and roughhousing on the playground, and the thought made her smile.

"Sounds like he was a wonderful baby brother," she said.

Jonathan nodded meekly as he took another sip of his coffee. "He was."

A moment of silence passed between them, and Andrea glanced across the room at the elderly man who was still sleeping in his chair, with a magazine draped haphazardly over his rather large belly. She could tell Jonathan was lost in thought, and she didn't want to interfere with that. Being an only child, she couldn't imagine the joy that must come from having a brother or sister...or the horrible pain of losing one.

"I never told him how much I looked up to him, and I regret that every single day. He was so great with Ben and Rachel, and I'll never understand why he wanted me to take care of them. I have no idea what I'm doing."

Andrea reached out and rested her free hand on top of his left arm, hoping it would comfort him in some small way. Even through the fabric of his long-sleeved shirt, she could feel the heat emanating from his body, which caught her off guard and made her knees weaken. Touching him probably wasn't the wisest thing to do, but she couldn't help herself.

"I don't have any children of my own, so I can't speak from experience, but I've worked with kids for several years now, and I can tell a lot about a child's home life by the way they act. Ben and Rachel seem like two very happy, well-rounded children, and I know their parents have a lot to do with that, but so do you, Jonathan. Don't sell yourself short."

He gave her a shy smile before setting his cup down on the window sill and stuffing his hands inside his pants pockets. "You've helped us so much today, and I really appreciate that," he said. "Thank you."

Andrea nodded as she took another sip of her coffee. Hopefully, he didn't notice the way her cheeks reddened in response to his sweet comment.

"Did you say your father *used* to be Amish?" he asked. "That's something I don't believe I've ever heard before."

She laughed softly when he cocked an eyebrow and gave her a curious look.

"He left home during Rumspringa when he was sixteen years old, and he didn't return. He doesn't talk about it often, but my mother said they met during that time, while she was visiting a friend here in Lancaster. They fell in love, and they've been together ever since."

He turned around and leaned against the window beside her. He was so close she could hear his steady breaths and feel the brush of fabric as their arms rubbed against each other. She breathed in deeply to try and keep her heart from racing out of control, but that was easier said than done.

"How did his family react...if you don't mind me asking? Do they still keep in touch?"

Andrea set her cup down beside her and crossed her arms over her chest. "His parents passed away when I was very young, and the only family he has left is my aunt Theresa – his sister. From what I understand, they haven't seen or talked to each other since the day he left. When I turned twenty-one I decided to look for her, and she and my uncle Luke welcomed me with open arms."

He smiled at her reply. "I can understand how he wanted to be with your mother, but I imagine it was also hard for him in a way. When Tom met my sister-in-law, Rebecca, and moved here, our parents were so upset."

Andrea gave him a quizzical look. "Wait...you're not originally from here?"

He shook his head. "We grew up in another order in Ohio. I didn't want to uproot Ben and Rachel from their home after their parents died, so I moved here to be with them."

Standing beside him, listening to him talk so lovingly about his niece and nephew, Andrea could almost glimpse into her father's past and understand a tiny bit of what he must have gone through. Jonathan Henning was selfless, compassionate, loyal...and not to mention, very handsome. He was making it difficult *not* to fall for him.

The realization made her heart skip a beat, but it also brought to light the fact that they came from two totally different places in life. She could never risk him being shunned from his community for seeing an English woman, and it wouldn't be fair to Ben and Rachel either.

They had been through enough heartache already during their young lives.

"Andrea? Is something wrong?"

She looked up at him, but she couldn't manage a reply as his piercing green eyes searched her own and held her mesmerized. She wasn't due to leave Lancaster for several more days, but perhaps it would be best to go home early and avoid what she was afraid might be happening.

Dr. Sloan opened the waiting room door at that time, and she breathed a sigh of relief at the welcome distraction. As they both walked over to meet him, she forced the troubling thoughts to the back of her mind so she could focus on the present situation.

"He's awake," the doctor announced. "You can go see him now."

It was the best news she'd heard all morning, and Jonathan's smile lit up the entire room, but she held back when he motioned for her to join him. Ben needed his family, and unfortunately, she wasn't – and could never be – a part of that equation. What she needed to do now was accept that fact and move on.

* * * *

Jonathan rubbed his eyes as the sun shone brightly through the hospital room window and woke him from a deep sleep. He was surprised to find Ben sitting up in the bed, munching on what looked like orange Jell-O.

"*Gute mariye*," Ben said with a smile.

Jonathan sat up straight in the reclining chair and rubbed his aching back. After tossing and turning for a couple of hours, he'd finally managed to find a comfortable position to sleep in, but the chair definitely wasn't meant for tall people.

He stood up slowly and stretched his arms and legs before walking over to the bed and placing his hand on Ben's forehead. He hadn't had any fever since the previous afternoon, but the doctor wanted to keep him overnight for observation, just to be on the safe side.

"*Gute mariye,*" he responded. "How are you feeling?"

Ben spooned more Jell-O into his mouth as he bounced up and down on the bed. "I feel great. Can we go home now?"

Jonathan sat down on the edge of the bed and lightly squeezed one of Ben's little legs.

"We'll have to wait and see what the doctor says, but hopefully he'll be discharging you today."

Ben emptied one plastic cup of Jell-O and quickly opened another. It made Jonathan's heart swell seeing him feeling so much better, and he felt like he could breathe normally again for the first time in two days.

"Where is Miss Andrea?

Just the mention of her name made his pulse race, but he didn't let on.

"She went home to check on Rachel and get some sleep, but she'll be here soon."

It was hard enough to fall asleep with her constantly on his mind, but relationships were unchartered territory where he and the kids were concerned. They had, after all, just lost their parents. The last thing he wanted to do was upset them by bringing a new woman into the fold.

"I like her," Ben said. "She promised to make me some oatmeal cookies as soon as I get home."

Jonathan chuckled as he watched Ben's eyes light up while he talked. A few minutes later a young nurse entered the room to check his temperature and other vitals, and Jonathan moved to the side to give her some room. He wasn't used to doctors and hospitals, and the constant beeping of machines and bustle of activity was hard to get used to. He couldn't help but wonder how Andrea dealt with it on a daily basis.

"Dr. Sloan is making his rounds, so he'll be here shortly," she said.

Jonathan nodded and thanked her before she left, and when the door closed behind her, he sat back down on the bed. Ben took one last bite of his Jell-O before throwing the spoon and empty containers in the trashcan beside his bed and resting his head on the pillow.

They were both quiet for a moment, and as Jonathan covered him with a warm blanket, he thought about the events of the past two days and sighed heavily.

"I'm sorry I didn't get you here sooner," he said. "This is all new to me, and I'm still learning."

Ben smiled and patted his hand. "It's okay, uncle Jonathan. I think you're doing a great job."

The compliment made him smile and brought tears to his eyes. The door opened again and Andrea walked inside, followed closely by Rachel, who ran into the room and jumped on her brother's bed and wrapped him in a hug. Their close relationship never ceased to amaze him, and he smiled as he listened to Ben talk excitedly about the doctors and nurses – and Jell-O.

Jonathan eased off the bed and joined Andrea by the door. The soft floral scent of her perfume drifted past his nose and made his knees wobble, but somehow, he managed to remain upright. She had on a red dress and sandals, and her long brown hair hung loosely around her shoulders. She looked absolutely beautiful, and the sight took his breath away.

"Did you get any sleep last night?" she asked.

He turned his attention to Ben and Rachel so she wouldn't see the goofy lovestruck look on his face. "*Yah*, I did. How was Rachel last night? Did she give you any trouble?"

Andrea shook her head. "She's a little angel. She was so worried about Ben, but aunt Theresa and I were able to keep her busy so she wouldn't worry. She begged me to come, and I hated to tell her no. I hope that's okay."

He motioned toward a small loveseat by the window, and they went to it and sat down. "It's fine," he replied. "Do you think there's a chance she'll get sick too?"

Andrea glanced at the kids and laced her fingers on top of her lap. "She should be fine. I'm going to leave you a bottle of medicine though, just in case she starts running fever."

Jonathan's heart sank. "You're leaving?"

She cleared her throat and shifted in her seat, but she wouldn't look at him. "I'll be heading to Laurel Springs as soon as I get you and Ben back home."

He opened his mouth to protest, but someone knocked on the door, a few seconds before Dr. Sloan entered the room. The next few minutes passed by in a blur, but Jonathan was able to grasp that Ben would be discharged within the hour. He signed a couple of papers and tried to listen as the doctor gave him instructions on what Ben should eat and drink once he returned home.

Andrea remained quiet the entire time, and when he happened to look her way, he caught her staring at him with an expression he couldn't fathom. Sadness, perhaps? He honestly had no idea. When Dr. Sloan left, he moved the chair and placed it directly in front of Andrea, so he could look her in the eye.

"Is this because of me?" he whispered.

He glanced over his shoulder at Ben and Rachel, to make sure they couldn't overhear their conversation, but they were jabbering away and oblivious to everything else going on around them.

"What are you talking about?" she asked.

He could tell by her expression that she knew exactly what he meant, but she kept her eyes glued to her lap. Jonathan leaned forward and grabbed her hands, and when she finally looked up at him, he could see tears glistening in the corners of her eyes.

"You told me yesterday that you would be here several more days, and now you tell me you're leaving. Unless there's an emergency back home I don't know about, I have the feeling it's because I've said or done something to upset you."

She squeezed his hands and gave him a half-hearted smile. Her skin was so soft and warm, and he couldn't imagine her not being near enough to touch anymore. Just the thought made his heart ache.

"When I decided to come visit, I never expected to meet someone like you, and I guess it caught me off guard."

Her confession made his heart race. "In a good or bad way?"

Andrea glimpsed toward the kids before sitting up straight in her seat and leaning forward so they were mere inches apart. He could see tiny gold flecks in her beautiful brown eyes, and her lips looked soft and kissable. He swallowed hard while struggling to maintain his composure.

"Jonathan, you and I both know what would happen if we started seeing each other. I don't want to ruin your life...or Ben and Rachel's."

He was surprised by her answer. "What makes you think that would happen?"

She expelled a long sigh. "I know what it did to my parents."

Jonathan caressed her hands before bringing them to his lips and tenderly kissing her fingers. Her eyes widened, and he noticed the way her breathing intensified, which spurred him onward. If she thought he would give up easily, she was highly mistaken.

"Andrea, that was a long time ago. And I've already told you I don't do things based on what others think. I follow my own heart, whether people agree with my choices or not."

She stole another glance at the kids. "And what about them? They've already been through so much."

Jonathan grinned. "Ben told me a little while ago that he likes you, and that's a big compliment coming from him. I'm sure Rachel does too."

She still looked unsure and so Jonathan scooted to the edge of his seat and held on tight to her hands.

"If you'll just give us a chance, I promise you'll see that everything will work out for the best. We can go as slow as you need to. I just...I just want to be with you, Andrea. I want the chance to get to know you and see where this will take us."

Her shoulders slumped as she looked down at their joined hands. "But I live two hours away..."

Jonathan lightly grasped her chin and lifted her head so she would look at him.

"One day at a time," he murmured. "That's all we can do."

When she smiled, it felt like a weight had been lifted, and there was a small glimmer of hope. They looked longingly at each other, and he desperately wanted to kiss her, but he knew it would have to wait until they were alone. At the moment he was content to just be near her, and he looked forward to finding out what God had in store for their future.

The sound of Rachel giggling interrupted the moment, and when he looked behind him, he caught her and Ben snickering as they watched him and Andrea talking. It made Andrea blush, but Jonathan took it in stride and laughed with them.

"Are you still baking me some oatmeal cookies when we get home?" Ben inquired.

Jonathan and Andrea stood and went to his bedside, and when she ruffled his hair and promised him two dozen cookies, he felt his spirits soar as Ben and Rachel bounced up and down on the hospital bed and clapped their hands together excitedly.

Andrea reached out and held his hand, and as the four of them planned their busy afternoon together, he couldn't help but wonder if Tom and Rebecca were smiling down on them from Heaven.

Something tugged at his heart and somewhere deep inside he knew...they were.

BENEATH THE AMISH SKY

NIKKI SALEM

<u>Chapter One</u>

She didn't love him.

She'd never love him.

Anna knew better than to think in absolutes, knew that she shouldn't assume she knew better than her father, but she would never love Samuel. Not if she was given a thousand years, not if he were actually closer to her age.

She was hardly twenty-one.

Hardly out of age for going to Sings and getting to court properly, her Rumspringa wasn't even finished.

Her father thought he knew what was best for her.

Samuel was an absolute nightmare though.

He was almost thirty-five, married once but his wife left to be English.

When Anna had first heard about this she felt terrible for him. It was horrifying to think that someone you pledged your life to could just leave you behind without a second thought. To live a life neither of you were familiar with. Anna couldn't imagine how selfish and cruel his ex-wife must have been. Leaving behind a chance at growing a family, at starting a life together, sounded outrageous-

Until she properly got to know Samuel.

His wife had made the right decision, and as she knew him better Anna began to envy the mystery woman who had flown the coup.

Samuel was boring, uninteresting, repetitive. He worked in the church, which her father found more than respectable, and so all he spoke of was the church. He went on for literal hours about repairs he wanted to do to the meeting building, hardly pausing to breathe. He didn't care to listen to her, or to stop once she was obviously uncomfortable. In all of the hours her parents had let him speak with her, she'd probably spoken less than twenty words.

She didn't want to have to live with that forever.

Anna couldn't imagine another sixty years, or more, of her life dedicated to this man who didn't care about anything but himself and the image the church gave him.

She couldn't see herself ever loving him, so marriage was a horrifying prospect.

The evening sun was just beginning to settle on the edge of the horizon. Her father had made up his mind, and all she could do was hope to dissuade him somehow. Gathering the last of the laundry for the next day, she listened for his tell-tale footsteps.

He was her father, she knew it was sad to be so nervous, but she was.

Sucking in a deep breath, she urged her feet forward, out to the kitchen where he was standing and drinking water.

"Father, may we speak?" she asked, her hands settled in front of her.

"Yes, what is it?" he asked, he was covered in mud from the day's work.

"I can't marry Samuel," she laid the words out neatly between them. Her father's mood seemed to immediately crumple into aggravation.

"You will," he replied back simply.

"Father I don't love him," she said, shaking her head. "He's so boring, I can't imagine a worse match," she admitted, approaching him.

"What does that matter?" her father asked, his voice raising. "You're supposed to be building a home and a family together, you'll love him in the end," he shook his head.

"I won't marry him," she said, standing her ground in a way she never had with her father.

"Are you saying my decisions aren't good enough for you?" he asked, slamming his hat down on the table.

"No, I-"

"You are my daughter, you had your chance to choose, that's over," he said sternly.

"I can still choose to leave," she said, hoping the words would bite him so he'd realize what he was saying. His face dropped into one of dark anger.

"If you will not listen to me, you *can* leave," his voice was like the grave, and it stung her.

"Father-"

"I will not have you speaking out against me, I make the decisions, I would rather have you married with him than unmarried with nothing but a dream of romance," her father was red faced in anger.

"Then I'll leave!" she shot back, the words slipped past her lips before she could catch them.

The air between them was still and quiet.

The moment stretched thinly, until a cough in the next room let Anna know her mother was nearby. She had a habit of listening in on conversations, and Anna couldn't hold it against her.

"I'll be gone by tomorrow night," Anna added, the words terrifying and unreal feeling even as she said them.

***

She didn't sleep that night.

Anna spent the night shoving what she could into a couple bags. Her clothing was plain, but plenty. She wasn't sure what she was planning on doing, on where she was planning on going. She just knew that if she spent another night under the same roof as her father she was going to explode.

Samuel wasn't an option.

In the blue light of morning she heard her father leave for his work.

Out her window she watched him pause for a moment, looking towards her window, and then step up onto his buggy and leave.

Just as well, she reminded herself, it would be easier to leave if he wasn't there.

As she started to drag her two bags to the front, her mother stopped her.

"Anna," her mother said, soothing a hand over Anna's right arm. "Are you sure you want to do this?" she asked softly.

"No," Anna admitted. "The only thing I'm sure I want in this world is that I do not want to be with Samuel," she explained.

"You could stay, reason with him, be patient with your father," her mother said gently.

"You know better than I do that's not an option," Anna sighed. "It's easier this way, otherwise I know I'd end up marrying Samuel," she explained.

"Alright," her mother replied. "You should take this though," she added, handing a small envelope to Anna. "It'll get you through long enough until you get a job," she tucked her arms tight around Anna. "You can always come back to me, my Anna, your father is stubborn but he'll miss you," she explained.

"He'll not want me back after this," Anna argued, feeling tears prickle at her eyes.

"You're his daughter, he always will have a spot for you," she countered,

"Thank you, mother," Anna sobbed, rubbing her eyes as the tears free fell.

"Of course my daughter," her mother answered, hugging her again. "I love you very much, I'll do anything for you to be happy," she added.

When her mother set to starting to clean laundry for the day, Anna was forced to start her journey.

The world looked too ordinary, too regular, for what day it was.

She steeled herself, and started her walk out of the village she'd always lived in. Out to where she knew cars would take her to a city, to a place so impossibly different and strange to her.

Anything was better than Samuel, though.

Chapter Two

Within her first week she'd already gone through over half of the three thousand her mother left her.

Anna was an intelligent girl, though. She'd found a room to rent in a Victorian home, something not too unfamiliar from what homes she was used to, for just a couple hundred a month. She paid six months of it in advance, and spent the rest on clothes, food, and a phone, to make herself to fit in.

Her new landlady, Holly, was to thank for most of the ideas and shopping.

She was a forty year old woman, and so kind, Anna was thankful she'd found her listing in the news paper. Not everything was as unfamiliar as she'd imagined.

People treated her differently, but as long as she ignored them they'd have nothing to say.

A couple men had talked to her, shown interest in her, but she had ignored all of them. She was sure she was being rude, she was sure that she'd never make any friends this way, but she also was sure that friendship wasn't what these men were wanting.

She'd never date.

Never go after any men, or marry.

She'd decided this on the ride out from her home.

Anna knew that she'd never find a man, an English man, who her parents would approve of. She couldn't marry someone they didn't approve of, even if she wasn't a part of the church anymore. In her heart she knew it would be the wrong thing to do.

She loved the idea of love, of finding someone who you match with perfectly, but she couldn't feel right being in that kind of love if it meant her family would look down on her for it.

She already had enough shame to bear.

The only thing left to do was to find a job.

Holly had gathered a list of places for Anna to look. Everything ranging from lawyer's offices, to factories that made holiday chocolate all year round.

She'd bought comfortable shoes, though, and she was happy to go to each business and try to impress with what she could. There wasn't much on her resume, but she had to try.

If not she'd have squandered her mother's money for nothing.

The general response to her from most companies was an extreme naked curiosity. They'd look at her like she grew a few extra heads during the conversation, and keep her there to talk to them for a bit. Just when she'd think she was closing the deal on the job, most places would apologize and say they were looking for someone with more experience.

She took that to mean they wanted someone who could operate a computer.

Her courage was waning, she wanted to get hired quickly, to be able to send her mother back a return of what she'd been given. Nothing was turning up, though, after a week and a half of, almost constant, searching.

Fearful for what was leftover of the money, not wanting to let herself have too much access to it, Anna found herself inside a bank.

The building was cold, refreshing against the summer sun, and empty besides her and a teller behind one of the long counters.

He caught her eyes, and a curdling guild set low in her stomach immediately.

He was gorgeous.

This stranger, with a name tag that shimmered out Andre, held her attention with more strength than Samuel had in any of the time she'd known him. His curly brown hair was combed back away from strong cheekbones and glittering green eyes. His shoulders looked broad, strong, and he seemed taller than most men she'd seen in the city.

When he looked up back at her, Anna felt chills run through her, and her face heated.

She didn't need to think about that, though, she was on a mission.

"Good afternoon," he greeted, setting aside the papers he was looking at. His voice was deep, echoing in the empty bank.

"Good afternoon," she mirrored. "I was hoping to open an account," she said, unsure how to phrase this. She regretted not asking Holly for help on this.

"I can help you with that," he smiled, turning to his computer. "Checking or savings?" he asked, typing.

"Checking, please," she responded, letting her eyes fall on his hands for just a moment before she looked away.

"Do you have two kinds of identification?" he asked, his typing stopped.

"Yes," she answered, pulling out the state ID she'd gotten just in the last week, and her birth certificate.

He accepted them and then froze.

"Are you Amish?" he asked, he looked stunned. "Or- were- you Amish?" he corrected himself, something nobody else had done.

"I was," she agreed. Her birth certificate named the only Amish town within a hundred miles.

"I was as well," he said, his eyes shining with nostalgia.

"You were?" she said, surprised for once.

"Yes, I was with a town in Idaho, I've been out of the church for five years," he answered.

"I just left the church almost two weeks ago," Anna said meekly.

"Well, welcome to the madness," he replied, a joke in his voice. She immediately felt comfortable with him.

This had never happened to her before.

"Thank you," she answered, unsure of the proper reply.

"I'll go ahead and set up your account," he started typing her information into the computer. "Will you want to use direct deposit for your job?" he asked, handing back her documents.

"I don't have a job yet," she admitted, embarrassed.

He typed something, and then paused for a moment.

"Have you applied here?" he asked.

"No," she answered, embarrassed at herself for overlooking the opportunity.

"We've been holding walk-in interviews, I can get the manager over to talk with you, if you'd like," he offered. "They're very happy to train, here," he said.

"That would be amazing," Anna said, surprised at her own luck.

As she watched him walk away, she could feel herself getting quickly attached. She knew she'd promised herself she'd stay away from boys.

She'd sworn she wouldn't date.

Still, she felt an attraction, an interest in him, that she'd never felt with anyone else. If she was going to live an English life, she owed herself to at least properly try it.

****

The interview was simple.

An older man, older than her father, asked her a handful of questions about her life an experience. He didn't seem phased that she'd never touched a computer until the last couple of weeks.

She stood up as the interview ended, expecting him to say they were looking for someone with more experience.

"Would you be available to start training tomorrow?" he asked instead, opening the door into for her.

"Yes!"

Chapter Three

Working with Andre was testing her convictions.

He was placed in charge of training her, helping her figure out the computers and the cash counting machines. Andre was patient, kind, and took his time with her even when customers were around.

She learned he'd moved into the state right after he left the church. He didn't own a television, but watched shows on a computer he had a home. She learned he liked to order lunch in, but always forgot to eat breakfast.

She learned he was incredibly generous with his smiles.

Regardless of how simple, how quick, her attachment to him had been within the first couple minutes of meeting him, it had grown into something stronger.

They bonded over talking about similar life experiences, over finding out what differences set them apart. He'd ridden in cars a lot growing up, none owned by his family, while she'd never been in a computer until the last couple weeks.

He was like a piece of her home that she'd left behind.

A warm blanket in the starkness of the new world she was getting used to.

A couple weeks into working together he asked her to dinner, and she couldn't make herself say no.

He picked a place close to her home, and she was both thrilled and terrified.

Holly immediately took the helm.

"I haven't dated in ten years, but you make me feel like I'm the one going out to night," Holly laughed, helping her pick out something to wear. "It's so funny that you're both Amish, isn't it?" she asked, Anna couldn't see the humor, but she nodded anyways.

"I think blue is really the best color for you," Holly said, pulling back Anna's hair so that it didn't cover the simple dress too much.

"Thank you," Anna said.

"But- are you sure you don't want to wear something brighter? Something turquoise and bright would really catch his eye," Holly offered, looking her over.

"No, for him I'd prefer to be myself," Anna smiled.

"Mm, alright," Holly tapped her shoulder, and Anna leaned her head back to let her braid her hair. They'd grown close very quickly, and Anna was glad to have someone in her corner. "He may be Amish, but he's still a boy, if you need anything please call me," Holly said, pausing to look Anna over in the mirror again. "You're gonna knock his socks off," she added, smiling.

***

The restaurant was busy when Anna arrived. She was early, so she requested a table, and then sat there and stared at the crowd.

She couldn't imagine what kinds of lives everyone in that building led. Jobs she'd probably never heard of, homes and cars that would blow her mind, problems she couldn't fathom. She couldn't imagine growing up in a world like this.

Anna listened to small snippets of conversations, catching foreign sounding ideas and words, until Andre arrived.

She was the one blown away.

He looked like he'd stepped out of a magazine. She was suddenly stunned to remember that he'd started out like her.

He'd integrated so well into this world that nobody around them would ever guess that he was Amish.

With her, she was sure people would figure it out.

He was amazing.

"Sorry I'm a little late, my Uber got lost," he apologized, sitting across from her.

"It's fine," she shook her head, smiling. She wasn't quite sure what an Uber was, but she told herself she'd ask him later.

The beginning of the date was jittery, she was nervous, and he seemed to be able to tell. She wanted to make a good impression, but was terrified that trying too hard would make her look like she'd forgotten her parents and church.

By the time they finished eating, though, she'd calmed down.

"Why did you leave the church, if I can ask," he said, stacking their plates he slid them to the end of the table.

"Oh, um," Anna wasn't sure how to explain it. She couldn't say she refused marriage, it would look like she'd never wanted to date anyone ever, but she knew she really wanted to date Andre. "My father and I had a disagreement, and he told me to leave," she explained, feeling shame at the explanation.

"Oh, I'm sorry," he said sincerely.

"It's fine," she lied. "I'm enjoying seeing what life out here is like," she admitted.

"I'm glad you're having a good time," he smiled. "So you'd rather be out here?" he asked.

"I'm not sure about that," she shook her head. "I just couldn't stay there," she tried to explain.

"Ah, I completely understand that," he agreed, take one last sip of his water.

"What about you? Why are you out here?" she asked.

"Mm, same thing, disagreements," he said. Anna wondered, her heart in her stomach, if he'd had a similar experience to her. She tried to picture him being forced into marriage, and the idea made her ache for him.

She was glad that his experiences led to him being in front of her, but was upset that it meant he had to be away from his family and the church.

"I want to go back, though," he admitted.

"Really?" Anna was surprised.

"Yes, of course, maybe not the same town, or the same people, but I miss the church. There's no sense of community or wholeness out here, I miss that so much it hurts," he explained.

"Oh," she said, surprised by him again.

She hadn't considered going back.

She'd only been gone a couple of weeks, and although she missed her family and connections she still felt better out in the world than stuck being married to Samuel. If he wanted to go back then her flirting with him was pointless. She wouldn't return with him and risk her father being disappointed in her.

Anna confirmed with herself that she was better off when she had sworn off dating.

When she finally decided this, looking back up at Andre he seemed concerned.

"What's wrong?" he asked, setting down his drink.

"Oh, nothing, I was just thinking about home," she lied.

"I get that," he nodded, continuing to eat.

She's have to stop seeing him.

Have to stop talking to him outside of professionally.

If he fell for her she'd end up hurting him and disappointing her family.

Anna continued to eat as she berated herself. If she was more thoughtful, more intelligent, she would have saved everyone a lot of heartache.

She'd tasted human interaction and became a glutton for it.

Chapter Four

It was harder to ignore Andre than she thought.

First of all, they worked together on every shift- which meant that he'd be within ten feet of her for most of an eight hour shift. Within the first half hour of their first shift together the following Monday he seemed to notice something had changed.

At first he spared her the embarrassment of asking her why.

They worked silently together, he helped her if she needed it, but kept his tone formal and plain. She did the same even though it hurt.

She wasn't sure why it hurt so much.

Anna hadn't known him for even a month, but looking at him and knowing she couldn't talk to him comfortably- knowing she couldn't hold his eye contact- anymore hurt her.

The first week of working together like this was like torture for her. He was a cold drink that her parched throat could never have. Their boss told them that their productivity was up and they had been doing a great job, and it was almost embarrassing. Had she been so distracted that she didn't work her best when she was talking to him?

Had she let him steal away her mind that much?

Anna was sure that the worst had passed. She was sure that he'd let go of his feelings for her, and she of hers, and that they could move on as regular coworkers. It wasn't something she was sure she wanted, and it hurt, but she told herself that it was for the best.

On the next Monday when she went in, someone was in Andre's spot besides him.

It was Kat, from the weekend, and some evening, shifts.

"Where's Andre?" Anna asked, trying to keep herself from seeming invested in the answer.

"He's out sick," Kat said, filling her drawer for the morning rush. "He called in last night," she added.

Anna's heart ached.

"What's wrong with him?" she asked.

"A flu probably," Kat guessed, shrugging. "Can you get me a couple more pens for my station before you get back here?" she asked.

"Yes, of course," Anna said, walking to the storage area.

He was sick.

He was sick and she didn't know? Her own stomach was turning and aching in fear. If she was over him why did it scare her so much just to hear he had the flu?

Why would she care so deeply?

Anna grabbed the pens and headed out.

She'd visit him after her shift.

***

Anna shouldn't have been able to get his home address.

She could have called him ahead and asked for it, but instead she asked Kat for help. If she called him her resolve would break. Anna just wanted to bring him some food and make sure he was okay. She wasn't going to stay long, she wasn't going to let herself say more than twenty words.

That's all.

She stood in front of his apartment complex, staring down the front of it like she was looking for answers.

Why did she care so much?

Why was a bag of hot soup and bread in her hand, why was she standing in front of a random man's home instead at her own home eating her own dinner? Why did it matter if he was okay?

At first she tried to convince herself that it was because he was Amish too, and that she was seeking that familial connection the entire Amish community shares. She knew that wasn't true. She knew better than to lie to herself.

Anna buzzed his room's number from the dial pad, and waited patiently.

"Hello?" he sounded sleepy and her heart warmed.

"I heard you were sick, I've brought food," eight words, she counted as she spoke them.

"I'll be right down," his voice chirped out quickly, like he was surprised. Anna was relieved he hadn't asked her to come up to him instead, she didn't want to appear to be straying any further from her convictions than she had.

"Hey," he said, opening the door after a minute. He looked ruffled, his hair askew and his shirt wrinkled. Her heart warmed at the sight of him, even when he was sick he was still handsome.

"Hi," nine words. She begged for her voice not to betray her.

"Come in, just to the lobby," he said gently, opening the door further. Anna knew she shouldn't but she did anyways.

"How are you feeling?" thirteen words. She could only allow herself seven more. If she went any further she didn't trust herself.

"A lot better," he said, fixing his hair with his hands. "I slept it off most of the day, drank a lot of tea and had a hot bath," he explained. "I should be back at work tomorrow," he added.

"That's good to hear," three words left.

"Yeah," he answered. Then paused for a moment and looked her seriously in the eyes. Anna felt like he was staring right into her mind. "How are you? You've been- different- this last week," he said. Anna considered her words carefully.

"I've been fine," she answered.

Twenty.

She needed to keep her mouth shut.

"Okay," he said gently. A silence hung between them, she knew he expected her to say more, she willed her mouth shut.

Anna handed him the bag of food, and then stepped back towards the door.

"Bye, then," he said, unsure.

Anna nodded, her hand on the handle to open it.

"Anna-" he said gently. She froze, not sure what to do. "Have I done something wrong? Have I hurt you in some way? If so, I'm sorry, I'll ask to be transferred to another location," he offered. "I've really enjoyed getting to know you, I'm sorry f I've made you unhappy," he continued.

Anna's hand tightened on the handle of the door as she felt her resolve start to unravel. He started to step away, and any less will power she had completely dissolved into the air.

"I can't go back and live there," she said softly, feeling tears prickle at her eyes. "I was foolish and got into a fight with my father, I refused to marry someone they wanted me to, and I ran off like a child," she explained, actually crying now. "You want to go back, and I can't give you that, I can't," she explained, shaking. "If I go back there my father won't care, he'll make me marry this stranger," she explained.

"Have you talked to him since then?" Andre asked, walking back to her. "It sounds like you both jumped into it quickly, have you talked about it?"

"I've only sent letters to my mother," Anna shook her head.

"I'm not even sure your town would accept me," Andre said gently.

"What?"

"Come sit down," he motioned to a couple chairs in the lobby. Anna nodded and wiped the tears from her eyes. She never thought she'd like him this much.

Never even considered it.

"I was forced to leave because my village was convinced that I stole something from a brother of mine, even though I was out of town when it happened," he explained. "He told them I stole and sold one of their horses to the English, and they believed him. I was made to leave within a week," he explained.

"You wouldn't do that," she gasped, disgusted someone would spread a story like that.

"No, I wouldn't," he agreed. "My brother was always greed, though, and my father just recently passed. Their house was to be mine, and now it's his," he said.

"That's awful," Anna shook her head, upset.

"It's how it is," Andre shrugged. "I won't make you go anywhere you don't want to, I won't make you do anything you don't want to, but please don't shut me out like that anymore," he said gently.

"Okay," Anna nodded, feeling drained and embarrassed.

He was too kind, too understanding.

"I want to speak to my father," she admitted.

"Want me to be there for it?" he offered.

"Maybe," she sighed, wiping the last of the moisture off her face. "You should eat," she added.

"Alright," he stood slowly, walking her to the door. "Thank you for talking to me."

"Of course," she said, feeling foolish for treating him how she did.

Andre leaned down and kissed her forehead gently, before opening the door for her. Anna could feel her heart rushing the whole walk home.

What did she want?

Chapter Five

She was in front of her home again.

Regardless of where she went, who she was in the world, this place would always be her home.

She'd waited the entire week, had pressured herself into patience as she tried to figure out what to say. She wasn't asking to marry Andre, he hadn't asked her, but she wanted to court him.

She wanted her parents to be a part of her life.

She couldn't silence how she felt about them, she couldn't hide what her mind was doing.

She just wanted them to know how she felt.

Anna plucked up her courage and knocked on the door for the first time in her life. Before this she'd always been able to just go in. Before now this was always where she lived.

It was evening, the sun starting to drip down onto the horizon as the air cooled. Long blue shadows painted the fields and homes, and in the glow she felt nostalgic. There were footsteps inside, and she waited patiently, her heart hammering in her ears.

"Anna?" her mother gasped as she opened the door. Anna was swept into her arms, pulled tight and close, and Anna could feel the shudder of her mother starting to cry. "I thought all I'd ever see of you anymore was letters," her mother sobbed out, clutching her against herself.

"No, no, I'm here," Anna answered, hugging her back. She could feel tears pricking against her own eyes. "I need to speak to father," Anna said gently.

"He has hardly spoken since you left," her mother admitted wearily.

"Then I just need him to listen," Anna replied. She felt like she'd aged years since she had been there last, even though it had been less than two months.

"Alright," her mother nodded, patting her arm and pulling Anna into the home.

The house smelled of dinner and dishes, her mother had been cleaning when Anna arrived, and it took all of her willpower not to distract herself into helping clean.

"Anna is here," her mother said as they entered the sitting room. Her father was there, the bible in his lap. When he looked up at her, his eyes seemed so sad. Her heart broke for him.

"Father," Anna said gently, moving to sit next to him on the couch. He watched her quietly, only breaking his silence to itch his beard. She could remember growing up and pulling on his beard as a young girl. He looked so old now. "I'd like to talk to you for a short while," she explained. He nodded, and glanced up at her mother, who then went back to the kitchen to continue cleaning.

"You're not wearing English clothing," he noted.

"I'm not English," she reminded him. It was good to hear his voice. "I want to apologize for going wild as I did, and not listening to you," she explained. "I don't regret not marrying Samuel, but I do regret arguing with you and disrespecting you." He was quiet as she spoke, listening to each word she said with immense consideration.

"I have met an Amish man while I've been out there, and I wish to court him," she explained simply. "I'm not here to beg you to accept him, or to tell you that I wish to marry him, I just don't want to keep any part of my life from you," she said. Her father nodded.

"Who is this man?" he asked, his voice was patient, not accusing.

"He's a coworker of mine at a bank, he's kinda and intelligent," she answered.

"He's Amish?"

"Yes, and he wants to join the church again and it will have him," she said. "I want to come home father, he wants to come with me, I miss my family and world," she explained.

Her father was quiet for a while, mulling over everything he just heard. Anna was patient and watched him carefully. Her mother walked by the outside of the room more often than was necessary, she knew she was listening for an answer as well.

Her father took her hand gently and stared down at it.

"Your mother has missed you," he said softly. She knew that he meant he did as well, she didn't question it. "When I chased you away like I did I was brash, I wasn't thinking about what was best for everyone," he explained. "I wanted you to have marriage, to have happiness, like your mother and I have found. I didn't consider that Samuel would ever make you unhappy," he continued. "I'll meet this man," he explained.

Anna reached forward and grasped her father into her arms. She hadn't hugged him in years, hadn't thought to, but she needed to hold her father. His arms wrapped around her as well, and she felt like a child again.

"I just want you to be happy," he said, his voice went weak for a moment, and she willed herself to ignore it. If her father cried, she's save him the embarrassment of knowing she'd seen it.

"I'm sorry I didn't treat you with the respect you've earned," she responded, holding him tight.

They sat there for a moment, reunited and feeling every inch of how apart they were.

"When can I meet him?" her father asked, leaning back away from her. There was a shine to her eyes that she felt her heart warm to.

"He's outside. He dressed in clothes he still had from his last town, he's waiting just outside of the fence," she admitted, bowing her head. "He requested to meet you both," she added. Her mother now stopped in the hall, no longer pretending she was carrying laundry back and forth for the tenth time. Setting down the basket, she approached the two of them and sat her hands on her husbands shoulder.

"We'll see him," her father said, nodding.

Anna nodded, and rushed out to get him.

"They want to see you," she said gently, pulling him out of his thoughts. Anxious nerves and excitement both crossed Andre's face, and she ached to wipe the lines of stress away.

"My father has forgiven me, we're okay now," she added, trying to soothe him.

"Alright," he said, taking her hand. "I love you," he added, the crickets around them were humming to life as the sun began to really set.

"I love you too," she breathed out, amazed that the words were hers, that she really meant them.

She couldn't fear anything, nothing was scary anymore.

She was in love, and her parents accepted it.

As she led him back to the house, her hand brushing against his, glad to finally be back home.

AMISH SUNSET

NANCY MANN

43

Chapter I

Rain decorated the grassy fields of Lancaster County. The sky was a cloud grey, the sun remaining absent as the county mourned for the loss of William Bradshire, a carpenter that had been known throughout the county for his kindness and love towards the people around him.

Friends and family had gathered in the county's cemetery for William's funeral, one of the mourners being William's love, Mary Lee Warner. Out of everyone there, Mary was the most damaged from it. William's parents had passed on early in his life due to illnesses and the remaining family he had weren't as close. If anything, Mary was the only one there who truly was family to him.

As Bishop David spoke about his memories with William, Mary thought to herself how God could do such a thing, to take away an innocent being this early in his life. William was only in his mid-twenties, like Mary. He had so much to experience in his life, but it was stripped away from him so early due to the accident.

"If anyone has anything to say, speak now." Bishop David said, stepping back and letting anyone step forward to speak.

There was a long pause, silence being present as Mary thought to herself. Eventually, she took a step forward, standing in front of the casket as she let out a depressed sigh.

"William...had a beautiful soul," Mary said quietly, holding onto a wildflower, "a soul that I have yet to find in any other human being."

Everyone was watching her speak, seeing what Mary had in her hand and what she had to say about William being gone.

"I can't imagine not meeting him in my life...all the memories we've made together...all the laughter, the love...I'm going to miss it." Mary spoke as tears ran down her cheeks. "I don't know if I will find another William in my life."

Some of William's family members began to have tears fall too as they listened to Mary's words about their lost kin. Mary soon stepped back from the casket, having finished speaking on the behalf of William's death. Bishop David soon stepped forward again, wiping some tears from his own eyes.

"Thank you Mary...I will say, before I close in prayer, that it will be difficult to find another William in our lives." Bishop David said to Mary before opening his Bible.

Verses from the Bible were soon spoken out loud, everybody bowing their heads in prayer as Bishop David spoke. While everyone listened, Mary wasn't listening to the verses, in fact, she was in her own mind at this point.

"Why God...why would you take William away from me?" Mary thought to herself. *"William didn't even get half way into his life...why would you take him now?"*

As she struggled with the idea of William passing on, Bishop David finished reading the verses, quietly speaking the word *amen* as he closed his Bible, everybody soon leaving the scene of the funeral, letting the casket to be lowered into the grave. While the casket lowered, Mary was the only one present, witnessing her love's final presence on the surface of Earth.

In regards to funeral traditions of the Amish, flowers were not placed on the casket. For Mary though, traditions meant nothing to her in this occasion. She took the wildflower that she was holding in her hand and tossed it down into the undug grave, letting it land on the coffin before the gravediggers began to bury the coffin.

"I love you so much William." Mary said as the coffin soon disappeared from the soil piling on top. Tears continued to fall onto the soil as she left the site of the funeral.

Chapter II

Several years later...the county had returned back to its normal ways, except for Mary. Ever since William passed away, Mary wasn't her old self. Her old cheerful personality had passed on as well, leaving her a closed up, emotionless woman in her mid-twenties.

She tried to return back to a normal life by going to church, seeing if God might be able to help her find peace, but the more she went the church, the more she began to question God. At times, she would find herself being angry at God for taking William away this early in his life. Eventually, Mary stopped going to church, which brought the concern of Bishop David, leading him to go to Mary's home.

Her house was a little way from town, being near one of the farms. She lived in a large house that belonged to William and his parents. Now that William passed on, Mary now owned the house and lived in it by herself.

Bishop David knocked on the front door, waiting for it to be opened. It took a few knocks before the door finally opened, Mary standing there in a stone grey dress.

"Yes?" Mary quietly said, looking at him with her expressionless face.

"May I come in?" Bishop David asked softly, his expression being hopeful that she would accept his request.

Mary let out a quiet sigh before she nodded, stepping out of the way for Bishop David to come in.

"Thank you...Mary." He said, soon walking into her home, looking around.

Mary shut the door behind Bishop David, walking past him and sitting down on a chair in the living room, continuing what she was doing before he knocked. When Bishop David sat down across from her, he noticed that she was knitting a quilt.

"Oh...I see that you've been busy with making a quilt." Bishop David said, giving Mary a gentle smile.

"Quilts. I've been busy making quilts." She said quickly, pointing in the corner to a basket of several quilts.

Bishop David was surprised by the amount of quilts she had made. "That's quite the number of quilts Mary." He said with a small laugh after.

Mary raised her eyebrows as she continued to knit the quilt. "I've found that work is one of the few things that keeps me from thinking about the past." She said softly, not making eye contact with Bishop David.

"Oh...well...if that's what helps you find peace." He said quietly, rubbing the back of his neck before he finally decided to talk about why he wanted to talk to her. "Mary...I'm worried about you."

She heard Bishop David, stopping for a second before she continued knitting the quilt. "Why?" Mary questioned him.

"I'm concerned for you because you haven't been going to church for months." Bishop David finally said, looking at her with a worried expression. "You were always an avid church-goer when William..." He said before realizing what he said, stopping in mid-sentence.

Mary immediately looked up when Bishop David brought up William, her knitting ceasing before she let out a sigh of disbelief escape her lips. She set the quilt and knitting needle down. "Please, do not ever bring up William to me again when comparing me to then and now." Mary said, her voice trembling as she had grown an upset expression.

Bishop David had become silent as he listened to Mary finally speak to him.

"I'm no longer the Mary from then because of the events that happened, and if you want to visit me and tell me how I use to love church and that you're concerned with me not being there on Sundays, then don't even speak, you're wasting your breath." Mary said to him, her eyes staring into his intensely.

Bishop David heard everything she was saying before he let out a sigh of sympathy. "I'm sorry Mary that you're like this...I didn't come here today to chastise you about not attending church. I came here because I'm really concerned for what you've become. I want happiness for you, I want you to have that cheerful personality that everybody knew you for." He said softly, standing up from sitting, looking down at her. "Always remember Mary, we all face events in life that we don't want, but it's all a part of God's plan for something greater."

Mary just glared at him the whole time he spoke, not even acknowledging the things he said. "I would like you to leave."

Bishop David heard her request and nodded softly, walking away from where they were at and leaving the house.

She had watched him leave through the windows before she finally reached for her knitting needles and quilt, continuing to knit as she thought about what he said about God having a plan for everyone. To her, God's plan was killing William and taking away something that she loved most in the world, when she didn't have anyone else.

"Forget God." Mary said to herself quietly, having completely lost faith and love in God.

Chapter III

One stormy night soon had arrived in Lancaster County. Rain had arrived over the town and fields, the sound of sharp pellets hitting the roofs and windows of each building. The window whirled between each building, the sounds of wind wailing could be heard by anyone who was awake.

While the storm stayed present in the county, Mary was asleep in her bed, although she wasn't sleeping soundly. The red-headed woman was having a nightmare, causing her to toss back and forth in her sleep before some sort of sound interrupted her slumber.

KNOCK KNOCK KNOCK

Mary sat right up from her bed like a vampire in a coffin, rubbing her eyes. "What on Earth?" She said to herself, looking around the room as she wondered what caused her to wake up.

KNOCK KNOCK KNOCK

This time, the red-head heard the solution to the noise. "Who could be at my door in the middle of the night?" Mary got out of her bed, wrapping her blanket around herself to cover her nightgown. She made her way down the stairs of her home before seeing the front door. Once she got to the door, she slowly opened it, seeing who it was.

There was a man, about her age, with a young daughter about six-years-old. They were wet from head to toe, shivering as they looked at Mary.

"Please...do you have room in your home for my child and I? We come from far away to Lancaster County...we have no home, no food." The man said, his tone being a desperate one.

Mary had no idea that this was what waited for her on the other side of the door. "I...Well..." She looked at the two before she finally nodded quickly, stepping out of the way.

"Oh thank you...thank you!" The man said happily and emotionally. He quickly moved inside, Mary shutting the door behind the two. Even though they were inside, away from the rain, they still were shivering in the dark home. Mary saw how cold they were and immediately knew what they needed.

She quickly went over to the fireplace in the living room, taking two logs that were on the side of the hearth in a pile and putting them inside the fireplace. After a few attempts of trying to get a fire started, she eventually managed to do so, an orange glow illuminating the living room.

Once the man saw the fire, he moved his daughter close to the fireplace, trying to get her as warm as possible. Mary saw what he was trying to do and quickly went over to the eight-year-old, wrapping her blanket around the child. The man soon began to dry off her daughter while at the same time trying to get her warm.

"There you go...nice and warm now. Away from the cold rain." He said quietly to his daughter, holding her close as he sat in front of the fireplace with her.

The daughter shivered still, but the warmth from the fire and the blanket caused the shivering to decrease as the time went by.

Mary stood behind the two, watching them and making sure that they were okay. "Are you warm enough?" She asked them, having held one of the quilts she had made in her hands to give to the man.

"Yes...thank you kind miss." He said quietly, holding his daughter close before taking the quilt from Mary, wrapping it around himself.

With the two warming themselves up from the fire, Mary decided to grab another quilt for herself before sitting down on her couch. She wrapped the quilt around her body so she could be warm too. Since she now had two "guests" in her home, she didn't want to go upstairs, back to bed, with the knowledge that two strangers were downstairs in her home, two people who she had no idea who they were.

"Maybe they're thieves," Mary thought to herself, studying the two strangers. *"Although...she looks pretty young to be a thief."* She finally decided to speak up, wanting to figure out who they were. "Where did you two come from?"

The man looked back at her, hearing her question before he began to reply to her. "We came from Somerset County." The man answered, still trying to warm up his daughter.

"Oh…that's far from here." Mary replied, sitting down on her couch, looking at the man.

"It very much is…" The man nodded, looking at her. "Do you know if there's any housing here in Lancaster County?"

Mary heard her question before she shrugged. "I'm not too sure. Are you looking for a place to stay?"

The man nodded, looking down at his daughter. She had fallen into slumber and had a warm expression on her face and had stopped shivering, indicating she was no longer freezing. "Yes."

She heard him and asked some more questions in order to get to know him. "Why Lancaster County? I'm sure there's plenty of other settlements along the way."

"I just," The man began to say, rubbing the back of his neck nervously, "I don't know…I guess I've heard a lot of great things about Lancaster. Figured that it would be a great place for my daughter to grow up in."

Mary nodded when he stated that it'd be a good place for his daughter to grow up in. "Lancaster really is a nice place to grow up in…a good place to start a fam-" she began to say before stopping when she was about to say "family." It reminded her of what she has always wanted to have and that made her think of William and her. "Well, it's a good place to meet nice and caring people."

The man saw her reaction when she was talking about family, but decided not to question it in order to remain polite. "That's good to hear…by the way," the man began to say, looking at her once again, "what is your name?"

She heard him and replied softly. "Mary...my name is Mary Lee Warner."

When the man heard her, he smiled softly. "That's a beautiful name."

Mary smiled softly when he complimented her name. "What about you? What's your name?"

"Robert." He said quietly, before looking down at his daughter, gently stroking her hair. "The little one is Miriam."

Chapter IV

The next morning had arrived, the rain was now gone, the only trace of rain being the puddles in the dirt. Mary decided to help Robert and Miriam out by going down to the church to see Bishop David could help them out.

Entering the church, there were only a few people present in the pews, praying to the Lord about whatever comes to their attention. Bishop David was not preaching, considering it was a Tuesday, so chances were he was at his home.

"Doesn't look like he's here." Mary said, turning around and leading Robert and Miriam out.

"Who are we looking for exactly?" Robert said, holding his daughter's hand as they walked towards Bishop David's house.

"We're looking for David, Lancaster County's bishop. He might be able to help you out with moving here." Mary replied, reaching the bishop's house before knocking on the door. Not too long after the knock, the door opened, Bishop David standing there.

"Mary?" He said, a little surprised. "What brings you here today?"

Mary explained the whole story to him, telling the bishop that Robert and Miriam showed up in the middle of the night, needing a place to stay and that they wanted to move to Lancaster.

"I see…" Bishop David said quietly, scratching his beard as he thought about it. "Unfortunately, there isn't any houses available right now."

Mary heard the news and let out a quiet groan. "So where will they stay if they don't have a home?"

Bishop David heard her before looking at the two, looking at Mary again. "Can I talk to you privately Mary?"

Mary was confused as to why, but nodded as she stepped inside the bishop's house. "What did you want to talk to me about?"

Bishop David looked at her before he let out a quiet sigh. "I wanted to talk to you privately about where they're going to stay. I believe they should continue living at your house until a new house can be built here in the county."

She listened to what he said before hearing his statement about the two staying at her home. "What? No. I can't have people living at my house."

Bishop David gave her a confused look. "Why not? You have one of the biggest houses here in Lancaster County. You're not living with anyone. There's plenty of room in the house for someone."

"Because, I don't have enough food to feed two more people. I don't want to start housing people." Mary was quick to say, folding her arms. "I can't let strangers come into my home and make themselves acquainted to the hou-"

"Mary." Bishop David interrupted, clearly showing he was getting irritated with her. "Enough with the excuses. I'm not going to force you to let them in. I'm only suggesting you give the two of them a home. It's not permanent, but where else are they going to go?" He asked Mary, looking at her with a serious expression. "They can't move into anyone else's home. They all have families, rather large ones too."

She listened to him, looking into his eyes as she thought about everything he was saying. Bishop David was right in many ways. Most families in the county had large families, homes that were already crowded. With Mary's house, it was just her. He even said that it wasn't permanent, so it'd be something that Mary didn't have to deal with for too long.

"I guess...I could have them stay for a little while." Mary finally admitted, realizing that she could be a little generous.

"Thank you Mary." Bishop David said before leading her back outside, now facing Robert. "We will discuss adding a house whenever I meet my colleagues. Until we can get a house added to the county, you'll have to stay with Mary for the time being."

Robert listened to what Bishop David said, nodding softly. "Okay, thank you."

Bishop David smiled softly, heading back into the house before closing the door.

Robert and Miriam turned toward Mary, looking at her. "So...are we going to back to the nice lady's house?" Miriam asked her father.

Mary heard her and couldn't help but smile. "Yes...yes you are."

Robert watched the two interact before he couldn't help but smile, seeing this stranger being so nice to his daughter.

"Alright. Let's head back to the house so I can get a room prepped up for you two." Mary said, clapping her hands together when she knew what she needed to do.

Chapter V

A couple of months passed by in Mary's household. The two strangers that had showed up on her doorstep were now friends of hers, having brightened up the household little by little. As Mary got to know Robert, he started feeling more and more comfortable around him, the two even joking around with each other.

With Miriam, she started to look up towards Mary as a mother figure, every now and then the little girl called Mary mom. Mary would hear this and laugh, finding it humorous that Robert's daughter called her mom.

While everyone was getting along just fine, Mary started to remember William again, every time she looked at Robert. There was something about Robert that reminded her of William. It might've been the way he made her laugh or the way he showed kindness to people. Whatever it was, Mary could see William through Robert, which made her think about if she found another William in her life.

It was now 6 PM and Robert and Miriam had finished eating dinner with Mary. When they finished, Robert decided to take Miriam to bed, since she started dozing off during dinner. Once she was in bed, she was out cold.

"She must've been really tired today. Miriam never goes to bed this early." Robert said, walking back into the kitchen. "I don't blame her...she didn't sleep that well last night."

"Oh poor thing." Mary said, cleaning the dishes in the sink. "I hope she rests well tonight."

"She probably will." Robert said, walking over before leaning against the counter. "So...what do you want to do?"

Mary continued to wash the dishes before she stopped, soon looking at him. "What do you mean?"

"Well I mean...Miriam is in bed early. Do you want to go out for a walk?" Robert replied, looking at her and waiting to hear an answer.

She looked at him before looking down at the dishes, thinking about his offer before setting the plates down. "I would enjoy that."

He smiled brightly before he walked out of the kitchen, planning on getting his jacket.

It didn't take long before the two were on an adventure, walking around the county in the early evening. The sky was an vibrant orange, the sun easing itself behind the hills.

"Wow...that's a beautiful sunset." Robert said softly, looking at it.

"It sure is." Mary said quietly, looking at it before she looked at Robert. With the two of them having grown closer, she soon started to think more in regards of making their relationship a bit more than friends. "Can I show you something?"

Robert heard her, turning his head and looking at her before he smiled softly. "Yeah of course."

Mary smiled brightly before leading him into the woods, walking in a certain direction. As for Robert, he wasn't sure where she was taking him, which made him a little nervous. Eventually, the two arrived in a rather large open area in the woods, a grass area that was decorated with wildflowers.

"Wow..." Robert quietly said to himself, stepping forward and starting to walk towards the flowers. "They're beautiful."

Mary stood behind Robert, watching his response before walking with him again. "I know. I love coming to this place. It reminds me of so many happy memories." She said before she began to lay down in the grass, looking at the sky that had become as orange as a Doris Longwing Butterfly's wing.

Robert watched what she did before he followed her actions, lying next to her as the two watched the sky. "You have quite the spot...especially one that you value." He smiled softly, relaxing on the grass.

The two watched the sky for a few, enjoying the time to relax with each other. Eventually, Robert spoke up, a question that had been resonating within him.

"How come you didn't want to let us live with you a few months ago?" He quietly said, still looking at the sky, some clouds gently moving along in the sky.

Mary heard him and gave him a confused look. "What do you mean?"

"You were talking to Bishop David the morning after the rainstorm. You told him that you didn't want anyone staying at the house because you didn't have enough food and didn't want housing people. Part of me though doesn't believe that."

Mary listened to what Robert was saying, her expression staying confused before her expression became more of a look of hesitant.

"There's something more than not enough food and not wanting to house people huh? You don't have to tell me, but just know I'm here if you want to talk." Robert said quietly, wanting to assure that she could trust him.

She listened to what he said before she began biting her own lip, thinking to herself before she let out a quiet sigh. "There is...there's a lot more to it. I think it's fair that you should know."

He heard her response to his question and turned onto his side, looking at her now as she began to speak about what the reason for not wanting anyone to live with her.

"It all has to do with a man I loved...a man named William." Mary said quietly.

Chapter VI

William Bradshire...a carpenter of Lancaster County. Most of the county knew him as the kind man who cared about everyone around him, even the ones who didn't care for him. William was the prime example of what it means to follow Christ's footsteps. He showed a strong love towards God, helped out around his community, showed love towards everyone, taught the youth about the Bible, and that's just the peak of the iceberg.

Sometimes in life though, bad things can occur that change one's life. For William, it was losing his parents at the age of eighteen. With his parents gone, he now owned the house, but that meant nothing to William. For a long time, he had struggled with the fact that his parents were gone, but during this time, he still continued to help people, having put them first before himself.

A great example of William putting others first was one cold, dark night. There was a knock on his door, the knock having echoed the entire silent household. When William opened his front door, he found a shivering girl his age, looking up at him. This girl was Mary.

The young girl had ran away from home, angry at her parents and her peers around her community. She was looking for a place to stay, which was she ended up on William's doorstep, a stranger to him. William was caring enough to immediately let her in; he even allowed her to stay as long as she needed. Even though she could've left any time, she found herself a priceless friendship.

Eventually, as time progressed, the redhead soon fell in love with William, the same happening with the boy. The two ended up revealing their love for each other when they discovered and rested in the grass area in the woods with the wildflowers. Ever since then, they were two peas in a pod.

As time progressed, they became closer and closer, almost being one soul. Mary began helping out in the community with him while developing a strong love of God since William introduced her to Him. Eventually, William decided that he was going to ask Mary for her hand in marriage, but his colleagues asked for his help in finishing the construction of a barn.

Unfortunately, William never had the chance to pop the question due to the accident. While he was watching his colleagues raise one of the barn walls up by pulling it up with ropes, the ropes snapped and the wall soon fell on William, his chances of escaping the wall very low with how fast the whole situation took. Sadly, William didn't survive the heavy barn wall crushing him.

Word soon got out around the county about William dying from the accident, which Mary soon heard about. She was devastated, crushed, her heart torn into pieces for the loss of her one true love.

After William had passed, Mary was given the house, considering she basically lived there and was a member of the community. During this time, Mary closed herself off from the rest of the world, locking herself away in her home, mourning the loss of William. She even decided to not let anyone into the house after the loss in order to keep the house peaceful, like it was when William and her were in it.

Even in the present, Mary still has nightmares about the whole incident, nightmares that remind her of the loss of William.

"If only I were there to stop him...to get him out of the way...If only I were there...he'd still be alive."

Chapter VII

Once Mary finished telling Robert the story, she had developed some tears from the memory of William's death.

"Now you know why I don't let anyone into the house...I know...it sounds insane, for the girlfriend of someone who has departed to keep the house like a temple. You must think I'm crazy..." Mary said quietly, wiping her tears.

"Oh no..." Robert said, looking at her. "I don't think you're insane at all...I can see why you value the house so much. All the memories with William...the laughter...the peace...everything about it...you don't want anyone to ruin this place for you." He said softly, gently resting his hand on hers. "I'm sorry...I didn't know this was the reason why you didn't want us here."

Mary heard him and finally broke down, tears rolling down her cheeks as she covered her face with her hands, muffled crying heard behind it. Robert reached for her and wrapped his arms around her, holding her close as he embraced her.

"Shhh...it's okay...Mary." Robert quietly said, stroking her hair gently to calm her down. "It's okay..."

After years of suppressing the memories of William and her, the pain she has endured from remembering his death, the many tears she had held back, she finally broke down and let her tears flow.

"I miss him so much...every day I wish I could see him again...tell him that I wish I could've saved him from the wall...I wish I could've done something." She said, pressing her face against Robert's shoulder as she shook from her crying.

"You couldn't do anything Mary...you had no idea that would happen..." Robert said softly, continuing to hold her close as she cried against him. "Look on the bright side...with William having a strong love for God, he's finally in Heaven where he can be with God...walk along with him...talk to him...laugh with him."

With Robert's words entering Mary's ears, it made her cry more. He was right in the sense that she wouldn't have known and that he's in a better place now. Her heart ached as she recalled all the memories of William from when they met to his death. All the memories were mainly happy and ones that would make her laugh whenever she looked back to them. Even though William was gone, she remembered one thing...William lives on through her. The memories, the house, the ideology, everything that William was made up of lives on through Mary. With this thought, she felt like she could finally get over the tragedy of losing William and achieve peace.

"Thank you...Robert...Thank you." Mary said quietly, looking up at him with tears in her eyes.

Robert looked down at her, confused as to why she was telling him thank you. "For what?" He laughed gently, wiping the tears away from her eyes.

"For saying all of those things about William and I...I've spent all these years holding onto William's tragedy and blaming myself for not being able to help him, but now I can finally find peace and let go of the tragedy...thank you...Robert." She finally said, looking at him as she gently reached up, stroking his cheek before she finally decided to lean in, kissing him gently.

Robert was caught off guard with the kiss, his eyebrows raising as she held her in his arms. Eventually, she broke the kiss, resting her head on his should. "Let's go back home...it's getting late." Mary said quietly, her eyes now closed.

Even though Robert had thought about pushing their relationship to another level, there was something that was holding him from reaching that level, something that had followed him from his previous home.

Chapter VIII

Many weeks had passed by since Mary told Robert about her past. Mary was in a much brighter mood, slowly building herself up again by socializing with people, going to church again, which made Bishop David happy, and she started wearing colorful clothes again.

Robert was thinking about what Mary had done in the wildflower area in the woods on the porch. He wanted to moved towards the next step, but the past was catching up with him.

"Hey!" Mary called out, coming up to the house with Miriam. "We've got dinner!"

He snapped back into reality, smiling gently when he saw the two. "Oh...that's wonderful. Looks delicious." Robert said, standing up and helping them take the food inside the house.

"I decided to cook something special for you...to thank you for helping me return back to my old self again."

Robert smiled and chuckled nervously, rubbing the back of his neck. "Oh...you don't have to do that."

"But papa," Miriam spoke out, looking at him, "look at the food! It looks delicious! At least let mom...Mary cook it for me."

Both Robert and Mary laughed at Miriam's comment, Mary picking her up and holding her.

"Okay, well if Robert doesn't want his special dinner, then I'll cook it for you." She said, walking in with the child.

"That'd be fantastic!" Miriam exclaimed happily.

Robert followed behind the two with the groceries, his expression being lost in thought as he thought about the past.

———

Dinner time soon arrived, everyone now seated at the table as they waited for Mary to come in with the special dinner.

"Whatever she's cooking, it smells delicious." Miriam said, excited to eat.

In a matter of minutes, Mary came out with a cooked turkey, the skin being a golden crisp.

Even though Robert wasn't asking for a special dinner, he was impressed with how the turkey came out. "Wow, looks really good Mary."

She smiled brightly, setting the plate down. "Well I'm glad you like it so much. I've got more coming out. I cooked some corn, made so mashed potatoes, have some greens." Mary explained to them as she walked back into the kitchen.

It took a few trips for her before she finally could sit down at the table with the two. "Alright, dig in." Mary said, taking her knife and fork, cutting into the turkey and scooping up a little bit of everything.

The dinner that they had all together was nice. Lots of laughter, lots of compliments, complete joy filled the room between Miriam and Mary, although Robert was most of the time quiet. After dinner, Miriam decided to go play with her doll in the living room while Mary and Robert were in the kitchen, cleaning the dishes.

While they were in there, Robert remained quiet, lost in his thoughts as he kept trying to shake it off. It didn't take too long though for Mary to see something was bothering him.

"You've been awfully quiet this evening...is there something wrong?" Mary asked him, continuing to wash the dishes.

"No." Robert said vaguely, not wanting to get into what was bothering him.

"You sure?" She said softly, looking at him. "You seem like you're thinking really hard about something."

"Don't worry about it." Robert said to her, trying to avoid explaining his thoughts.

Eventually, Mary let out a quiet sigh before setting her dish down, turning toward Robert.

"You know if something is troubling you, you can te-" Mary began to say to him.

"Drop it." Robert said harshly, looking at her for a few quick seconds before he finally set his plate down, shaking his head. "Just forget it...I'm going to bed." He said, leaving the kitchen and walking upstairs.

Mary was shocked by the way Robert reacted, considering it wasn't normal for Robert to be this way.

Miriam heard the commotion from the living room, looking at Mary. "Is papa upset about something?" She said with a concerned voice.

Mary heard Miriam and shook her head. "Don't worry about it dear. He just needs some time to himself."

Chapter IX

Robert currently laid in Mary's bed upstairs, his eyes closed as he tried sleeping. He didn't mean to snap at Mary, but considering his thoughts were getting to him, it was bound to happen. As he attempted to sleep, he soon felt something lay next to him, which interrupted his slumber. He opened his eyes and turned to look and see if it was Mary.

Of course, he was right in this situation. Mary was in her nightgown, having crawled in bed with Robert, getting cozy. Once he saw it was Mary, he returned back to his previous position, his back facing her. Still trying to avoid breaking the news to Mary, he soon felt her arms around his stomach, her body soon pressing against his back.

"What's going on with you? You're usually not like this." She said softly, resting her head against his back.

"I don't know Mary...I don't know." Robert said quietly, his eyes still closed.

"I feel like you do know Robert." Mary finally said. "I just feel like you don't want to tell me what you're thinking of."

He heard what she said, but didn't reply to it. The only thing he did was sit in silence with his eyes closed, trying to fall into slumber.

"You know I'm here if you want to tell me what's bothering you. I think it'd be healthy if you did though because you won't get any sleep with you thinking about whatever you're thinking. I know from experience." Mary quietly said, now closing her eyes as she rested her head against his back.

Robert listened to what she was saying before he let out a quiet sigh, trying to think about how he would explain his thoughts to her. Eventually, he decided to be straightforward with her.

"You know why I decided to move to Lancaster County?" He asked Mary quietly.

She merely shook her head against his back, indicating that she didn't know why he moved here. "Aside from finding a new home, no I don't."

Robert listened to what she had to say before he continued. "I left my previous home because my wife walked out on Miriam and I."

When Mary heard this, her eyes opened up and she sat up, looking down at him. "What? That's horrible! Why would she do that?"

Once Mary sat up, Robert turned so that he was laying on his back, now looking up at her. "To be honest...maybe I married the wrong person. She just...everything seemed fine to me. She was a good mother, I was a good father, we lived a happy life, but then one day..." He said before stopping, thinking back to that day before telling Mary what happened.

———————

"Sara?" He called out, looking around his home. "Where are you?

While he walked around the house, Miriam watched him, not understanding what was going on. "Papa? What's going on?"

"I can't find mom. She's gone." Robert said, his tone being a little more scared. "Maybe she left something saying where she went. Yeah...she leaves notes."

"Maybe...I'll help you try and find something" Miriam said, getting off of the couch before walking around their home, trying find anything that could lead to the mystery of where Robert's wife went.

Eventually, Miriam found a note that had fallen on the side of the bed. "Papa!" She called out. "I found a note!"

Robert immediately ran into the room, seeing the note in Miriam's hand. He took the note from her and began reading it. Although the hope he had on his expression when he found the note soon faded the more he continued to read it. In fact, he soon had become emotionless from what was written on the note.

"What does it say papa?" Miriam asked, looking up at him.

Robert finished reading the note, looking down at Miriam before folding the note in half, tucking it into his pocket. "Don't worry about it sweetheart. I think though...we need to move away from this county."

When Miriam heard this, she was completely confused. "Why? Why do we need to move?"

He heard her before he picked her up, looking around the house one last time. "Because I think we will find somewhere else that'll be better for the both of us."

———

"We basically left the county with nothing but the clothes on our back. I couldn't stand living in the same county as her and live in a house that we lived in together." Robert said quietly, looking at Mary as he finished explaining his story. "Would you stay in the same place if you found out your love left you and your child for someone else?"

When Mary heard this, she let out a depressed sigh. "No...I don't think I would." She said quietly. "Is that what's been on your mind today?"

Robert heard her before nodding softly. "I've been thinking about it for a long time now...I've wanted to move onto the next step in our relationship, but...I fear that something would happen again...I fear the odds of you walking out on us."

Once Robert said that, Mary spoke up in a more serious tone. "Robert...look at me."

Robert did as told and look into her eyes, seeing what she would say.

"I would never do that...ever in my life." Mary said, looking at him as she gently rested her hand on his cheek. "I wouldn't do something to hurt you and Miriam...I love you both, with all my heart." She said to him before she gently kissed him, breaking it soon after before resting her head on his chest. "You don't need to worry about me every walking out on you two...I care about you two so much that my heart aches. I wouldn't even think about walking out on you two."

When Robert heard this, he let out a relieved sigh, his arms wrapping around her and hugging her against him. "I love you so much Mary..."

"I love you too Robert..."

THE END

LOVE UNLIKELY

Chapter 1

Haylee lay in the darkness of her room staring out of the window at the moon that hung low in the sky, her only consort in her lonely life of misery and depravity. Four years after meeting Jase her heart was broken into a million pieces and scattered across the vast expanse of her own insignificant universe. *Move on,* they said, *he's not worth it,* they said, *you deserve better.* What did they know? None of her so called friends could ever imagine how she felt deep down and how utterly destroyed she was when she walked in on Jase in the arms of her best friend, Lucile. Of course the first thing both of them shouted when caught in the act was – *it's not what you think!* – The most default response.

After Jase pleaded with her and Lucile convinced her that it was an irresponsible judgement error on her part and that it would never happen again, she gave it another shot. She should have known better. Naïve little Haylee, who only tries to see the good in people ended up as the biggest fool of them all and when it happened a second time, she could no longer be ignorant. It was obvious that between the chemical combination of Lucile's raging pheromones and Jase's ego boosted testosterone, she never stood a chance. She had to finally admit to herself that she was never going to find true love, and friendships are feeble pastimes for pre-schoolers.

It's been almost two months since her relationship with Jase ended, and it wasn't long after that, that she also handed in her resignation as an article clerk. Breaking up with Jase and seeing him once in a blue moon she could handle well, but working with him and sharing the same open office day in and day out was a little too much to handle. It amazed her how men in particular, could be so callous and move on without a worry in the world. She had managed thus far, but the more she sat at home she started to feel cooped up like a bird in a too small cage.

She sighed and tugged her blanket over her shoulders and tucked it under her chin as she turned unto her other side, this time staring at her graduation photo. She stood tall and proud, alone in her toga with her rolled up certificate in her hand, no immediate family to share her successes with her. Her mother, or rather adoptive mother had passed away six months short of her graduation that year. Haylee sniffed and blinked away the tears. She didn't cry then and she won't cry now. Finally giving up on sleeping she tossed the blanket back and sat up in bed. Her mom always told her, that every person has left something behind in their past, that sits there and waits until they go back to find it and resolve it. And until recently she had never thought she wanted to go back there. She was only four when she was adopted, a lonely grey mouse stuck in foster care. From the first day she arrived at her new family, she was accepted and spoiled rotten. She never needed for anything in her life, and she never felt as if she was any different to any of the other kids, so why she suddenly felt like digging out the past was a mystery to her, but every day it became more and more pressing. And here at two in the morning, she was stuck between forcing herself to sleep or logging into her email to see if the adoption agency managed to track down her biological mother or family. Insomnia won the battle and she finally made herself a cup of coffee and sat down at her desk and logged into her emails.

Dear Miss Jones

We have managed to track down your biological mother, but it is with regret that we inform you that she passed away a few years ago due to illness. We have however managed to track down her parents, your grandparents. We do however wish that you consider the fact that they may not...

Hayley stared at the email, reading it over and over again, somehow grief evaded her, and it was like reading the sad story of a stranger. What she did learn from this was that her mother was born Amish, and that her grandparents lived in an Amish community in Ethridge,

Tennessee. But even if she knew who they were, what good would that do now? It wasn't as if she could reunite with her long lost mother anymore. But what she might be able to figure out is what type of woman her mother was and what type of life she lived. Maybe it will even shed some light on why her mother gave her up for adoption. As she spent her time reading up on the Amish and their culture, it became more and more evident that her mother may not have had a choice, but this was pure speculation. And unless she took the time to find these things out for herself, she would always be guessing about the woman who brought her into this world.

Besides, it wasn't as if she had anything better to do with her time. She had no job, no love life and no coffee, she thought as she looked at the empty canister in front of her.

That was it; she was going to take the last of her savings and head to Ethridge and find the Lapp's.

Chapter 2

The whole way to Ethridge, Hayley kept wondering if she was making a mistake. She was about to embark on a journey she was in the least bit prepared for. Before she left everything behind, she made effort to reinvent her wardrobe with a few modest outfits just so that she wouldn't look too outrageous amongst the Amish. But even now as she sat in the back of the cab, her heart was beating a million miles a second and she was on the verge of having a nervous breakdown. She had just left behind the only life she knew, not that there was much left of her for her to salvage, but she was somewhat comfortable where she was.

The cab pulled into the small town of Ethridge and stopped in front of what appeared to be a touring business.

"This is as far as I can go missy," the cab driver said and pointed to this meter.

Hayley nodded and fished for cash to pay the cab driver and the moment her bags were offloaded and she stood like a singled out deer in hunting season outside on the sidewalk she wanted to burst out in tears. Whatever was she thinking coming out here?

"Hello, may I help you?"

Startled Hayley nearly lost her balance as she spun to look at the stranger behind her, "Oh-I-um, well, I'm looking for someone," she said and dug in her purse, "Mr and Mrs Lapp?"

"Oh Fredrick and Mary Lapp, *yah*, they live here. I can take you," the young man said.

"You know them?" Hayley asked in disbelief.

"Yah, well it's a small community we all know each other," he said tucking his thumbs under his suspenders.

Hayley couldn't help but stare, wondering if all Amish men were this good looking. This guy couldn't be much older than her twenty five. And although he was dressed modestly in what she had to assume

Amish clothes, he looked reasonably attractive. She was never one for men with hairy faces, but for some reason his beard which was slightly trimmed suited him perfectly. He had ebony black hair with willow green eyes set deeply in his skull.

"If you're done staring..." he said interrupting her thoughts with his brows drawn together.

Embarrassingly she shook her head, "I'm so sorry, I just... it has been a really long day and I've travelled a long way."

"No matter, my name is Duncan," he said and nodded his head courteously, extending his hand.

"Hayley," she said and gave his hand an overly firm shake.

"Well I best be getting you to the Lapp's, the weather is turning foul."

Without notice he started loading her luggage into a carriage that stood nearby and then patted the back of the carriage, indicating her seat.

Who was she to ask questions, she hadn't the foggiest about their customs and every website she visited to learn about them were know-it-all windbags who have made up assumptions. So instead of opposing she hopped into the back of the carriage and sat down.

"So do you know the Lapps?" Duncan called over his shoulder as they made their way into the town.

"I...sort of, actually, I knew their daughter," she lied, she had no clue what their daughter was like. Just because Hannah Lapp gave birth to her, didn't exactly mean she knew her.

"I think you might have them mistaken for someone different, they only have a son, but Kendrick moved to Lancaster with his wife."

Well this was a good start, she thought as she tucked her lip under her teeth, "Perhaps I am confused, but I suppose there is no harm in meeting them. Maybe they might know Hannah Lapp as extended family."

"Hannah Lapp," Duncan repeated, "The name sounds familiar."

The carriage came to a halt and Hayley fell forward along with her luggage and just then the heavens opened up.

"Come!" Duncan called and reached for a sheet to cover her luggage before effortlessly lifting her off the wagon and placing her on her feet, "The Lapp's live here, if you hurry I can wait and take you back to Richland Inn."

"Wait, what do you mean back to town, I need to be here in Ethridge," she protested as Duncan lead her up to the house where the Lapps lived.

"Well if the Lapps won't let you stay in their home, you have nowhere else to stay, unless you want to sleep in the barn."

"The barn?" she asked appalled.

"Duncan, *vas in der velt*?" an elderly man interrupted as he opened his door.

Duncan immediately removed his hat and clutched it in front of him then looked at her before turning his attention back to the older man.

"Mister Lapp, this is Hayley. She's come to Ethridge to look for..."

Before Duncan could continue Hayley stepped up and extended her hand, "Grandfather?"

The older man's complexion paled, and he exchanged looks with Duncan then looked at Hayley, "You're mistaken," he mumbled and moved to close the door, but then an elderly woman appeared and the expression on her face was one of pure shock.

"Hannah... you look just like her," she said in a trembling voice as her eyes shot full of tears.

"Grandmother?" Haylee said as she stood with her hands folded in front of her.

"Come dear child, you're going to get soaking wet out in the rain," she said as she dragged Hayley into the house, despite her Grandfather's disapproval.

And as she disappeared into the kitchen she heard her grandfather mumble for Duncan to bring her luggage inside.

Her grandparents, she couldn't believe it. She was actually in the very house her biological mother grew up in. Her grandmother seemed far more accepting of her than her grandfather did, but she refused to make any assumptions until she had all the facts. For now she will take the time she had to get to know them.

Chapter 3

A week since her arrival and all she could determine was that her mother, Hanna Lapp went on a Rumspringa and never returned.

"Did she never write to you?" Hayley asked her grandmother one morning after her grandfather left to go to work.

"She wrote to us, but only ever to let us know she was fine," her grandmother said softly as she continued with her sewing.

"But weren't you in the least bit worried?"

Mary put down her sewing and reached out for Hayley's hand, "Yah, we were worried, especially your grandfather, but our laws are different to those on the outside. Hannah made her choice and she had a chance to return."

Hayley sat quietly for a moment and squeezed her grandmother's hand. The short while she had been here in the Amish community of Ethridge, she had found a sense of peace and tranquillity she never felt before. With the exception of a minority of locals who walked wide circles around her, the younger people like her were friendly and very accommodating. She couldn't understand why her mother would have left for good, and trade this life for what lay outside in the world. But then, being on holiday in a strange place was far different that living the life in full.

A knock on the door drew her attention and her grandmother quickly set her sewing aside and went to open the door, and a few seconds later she returned with Duncan in tow.

"Hayley, Duncan is here to see you," her grandmother said smiling.

Duncan was another person she was growing fond of at an alarming rate, but thankfully the walls she erected around herself kept her level headed. She knew that the only reason she felt closer to him than any of the others was because he was the first person she met when she arrived.

"Hi Duncan, what a nice surprise," she said standing up.

"Good day to you Hayley," he nodded tucking his thumbs in his suspenders, "I was wondering if you would like to go to the market today, I have a few errands to run."

Hayley felt the slight flutter of butterflies in her stomach and tugged her hand into her midriff. It would be rather nice to get out a little and get to know other parts of the community, she thought and then nodded.

"It would be lovely, let me get my coat and purse," she said and hurried to her room.

She forced herself not to eavesdrop on her grandmother' and Duncan's conversation and quickly got what she needed before joining them.

In no time they were on the carriage and on their way to the market, this time Hayley got to sit in the front and not like some baggage on the back.

"So how are you enjoying your stay here in Ethridge?" Duncan asked curiously.

"It's nice. I mean, it's very different to city life, but so far I'm enjoying the peace and quiet," she said and glanced out over the landscape.

"Yah, it's very quiet. So did you manage to find out about Hannah?"

"A little," she said, but decided not to elaborate. She didn't want to put the Lapps in any sort of disrepute, but she found it hard to believe that Duncan had no clue about her, but then again, he was probably still a baby when Hannah left the Amish community.

"So will you be moving on then?" he said clearing his throat.

Hayley turned to look at him and smiled, "Not sure, maybe. Tell me about this Rumspringa thing."

Duncan laughed and looked at her, "Well, Rumspringa means to run around, when the youngsters turn sixteen they can choose to go out and experience things outside of our community. It's each one's choice, some do it and some don't."

"Did you ever, I mean did you do it when you turned sixteen?" she asked curiously.

"Nay, I never did. I have all I need right here."

"So you never wonder what lies out in the cities."

Duncan drew the carriage to a halt and then turned to look at Hayley, studying her with those intense willow green eyes.

"Most young men leave because they are not satisfied with their life here, mostly because they are tempted by the modern world, and women," he said and for some reason his cheeks grew rosy.

Hayley tried to hide her smile and coughed softly, "So you never wanted to go find some hanky-panky?"

"Hanky -panky?" Duncan asked and blinked, "What is that?"

"Uh... well meeting women, dating and so on."

Duncan threw his head back and laughed, "Oh no, I had no interest in those things. Not then anyway," he said and then tugged on the reins sending the horse back unto the road, "I always believed that at the right time God will send the right woman my way. I'm a patient man Hayley Jones."

When he looked at her then, she felt her heart flutter in her chest and she immediately looked the other way. Her mind was clearly playing tricks on her; there was no way that Duncan would even consider looking at her twice. She was an outsider for one, and secondly she wasn't exactly a virgin either. And although she still knew very little about their laws and traditions, she was sure the Amish probably had the highest moral values in the world second to nuns.

The rest of their trip was in silence, and a few miles further they finally reached the Amish Country Mall. Hayley was quite surprised by the variety of goods that were sold at this place, but more so how many non-Amish visited the place. It was like a tourist distraction for curious people. And as she stood next to Duncan and the Carriage in her own authentic Amish dress, a sense of pride washed over her. Surprised that she actually felt Amish in some farfetched way, she smiled at Duncan and then headed into the shop. She found it quite amusing that it was called a Mall when all it really had were old antique trinkets and a limited menu of food. There were some items for sale but it was hardly considered anything close to a shopping Mall. She did her bit to get a few items for herself and when she next exited, she found Duncan standing next to her grandfather, both in deep conversation. Instead of barging in on them she took a walk around the store to give them their own time. Her grandfather had hardly spoken a word to her since her arrival and he was still a great big mystery to her. On occasion when she did ask her gran about him, she simply avoided the topic. She wasn't any closer to find out exactly why her mother never came back.

Chapter 4

Duncan couldn't help but admire Hayley, and although she was an outsider, she seemed to adapt quite well to the Amish life. It's been two weeks since he met her, and the more time he spent with her the more he started to like her. The first day he saw her was the first time he ever really looked at a woman. She was modestly dressed in a floral print dress that flowed elegantly down her body to her calves, but what intrigued him most was her shyness. The fact that he had the impulsive need to run his fingers through her long brown tresses was abnormal for him and he quickly stifled that need, by reminding himself that she was an outsider, which helped.

Normally when outsiders visited the Amish communities they stuck to their modern clothes, where the women wore as little as possible. No wonder so many of the Amish boys opted to go on their expedition to the cities, being tempted by the promises that the modern world presented. Two of his own best friends went out to experience the world and all it had to offer, but he never felt that desire or pull to know what happens out there. He was more than content to live this life of simplicity, working on the farm and making goat's cheese. There were many times when he attended the sings and where he contemplated the option of taking a wife, but none of the girls here in Ethridge ever made him feel the way he did now. And he was adamant that if he was going to take a wife, it would be someone who would completely consume his thoughts. He wanted the same love with a wife than his mother and father shared. He had never seen them argue, and they always showed their affection towards each other. And if they could have such a devoted marriage, why could he not have the same?

Duncan was caught in his own thoughts when the smell of burning wood and grass wafted through the air.

"Duncan!" It was Hayley who rode towards him on one of the Lapp's horses, her eyes wide, "Come quick, my grandfather's barn is on fire!" she cried.

In an instant Duncan had called his father and his neighbours, and everyone else he could alert and they were on their way by carriage to the Lapp's farmlands. Up ahead he could see the plume of fire explode into the grey sky. Flames rolled outwards and embers were flying up into the sky.

When he pulled up next to Hayley where she dismounted the horse, he took the reins and handed it to another young man, "Take the horse to my father's barn and keep it there," he instructed and then turned to Hayley, "What happened?"

"I have no idea, we were all having dinner when we heard the loud crash of lightning, and not long after that the smoke was everywhere," she said ringing her hands together.

Duncan's concern for Hayley had to be set aside, and although he wanted to comfort her, he had to attend to the bigger problem.

"Okay, go to the house and stay inside," he ordered as he scooped a bucket of water from the trough.

"But I can help," she protested and reached for a small barrel.

"You've done enough, now go and sit with your grandmother, I'm sure she could use the company."

Her mouth opened in protest but then shut, and with a slight nod, she ran across the field towards the house.

They fought all night to get the fire under control, thankfully the Lord had blessed them with rain to help put the fire out, but all that was left were the charred remains of the barn in the smoky morning air that reeked of burnt wood and straw. His father had warned Fredrick about the tall dead tree that stood so close to the barn. But misfortune led to lighting striking the dead tree and causing it to fall on to the barn. Luckily it was only the barn that burned down, somehow the horses were freed before the barn was completely on fire, and he has the slightest suspicion that it was Hayley's quick thinking that saved the animals. As for the equipment, it was all replaceable.

"Thank you son, if you didn't arrive when you did I would have lost all my horses," Mr Lapp said as he came to stand next to Duncan.

"Nay, that was not my doing. Hayley saved the horses," he said and looked at the older man.

"Hayley saved them?" he asked disbelievingly.

"Yah, she came to fetch me on horseback, I've never seen a woman ride so well, but she came to call me straight away. By the time I got here the horses were already in the fields and Kent took them to my barn."

Fredrick stood quietly for a while rubbing his beard, and Duncan knew that he had his own demons to face. He too had never heard of Hannah Lapp, but spending time with Hayley he had learned a great deal.

"She's seeking your approval," Duncan said crossing his arms as both of them looked at what remained of the barn, "She deserves a fair chance."

"You're right," Fredrick said and then headed towards the house.

Duncan looked as the older man walked away, his shoulders hunched as if he carried a heavy burden, but he knew Hayley deserved a fair chance, she had nothing to do with her mother's disobedience or her choice to give her up for adoption.

Later that day, Duncan stood in his father's barn, grooming the Lapps' horses. The least he could do was make sure that none of them were injured. But more than anything he needed to keep busy so that he could chase the thoughts of Hayley from his mind. Every waking hour was seemingly consumed by thoughts of her, and after her courageous act it was even worse. Now he knew exactly how King Solomon must have felt, being tempted by a beautiful woman.

"Duncan?" he heard Hayley's voice from outside the barn.

"In here!" he answered and tossed the brush in the sack hanging on the wall.

"Oh there you are," she said smiling and held out a basket for him, "Grandma and I baked these to thank you for helping us out with the horses."

Duncan smiled and took the basket filled with cookies, "Thanks, but I think you deserve all the credit, if it wasn't for you these horses would be charred with the barn."

He noticed Hayley blush as she averted her eyes, "I love horses, I had to do something."

Duncan stepped closer and reached out to tuck his finger under her chin, "And you did an amazing job of saving them," he said but his voice betrayed him.

This close to her, he could smell the fresh scent of lavender and vanilla, and although it was just the crook of his finger brushing her unblemished skin under her chin, it was the silk soft smoothness that tempted him more than anything. And without a second thought he stepped in and pressed his lips against hers. Hers were soft, like cotton pillows and although the kiss was brief, it was a defying moment for him. He knew there and then that Hayley was the woman he'd been waiting for all these years.

He broke the chaste kiss but didn't step away from her; instead he kept his eyes locked on hers. It was that moment between two people where words were irrelevant syllables and consonants were fleeting sounds that would never be able to express the emotions that sparked between them.

It was Hayley that stepped away first, and how shyly tucked a strand of hair behind her ear.

"My grandfather said that they will be doing a barn rising this coming weekend, will you come?" she asked softly.

"I wouldn't miss it for the world," Duncan said.

And as Hayley walked back out of the Barn she looked back over at him again and smiled.

Duncan felt like a teenager for the first time, and now more than ever was he determined to make Hayley Jones his wife.

Chapter 5

The barn raising was well on its way, the men from the community had spent most of the morning working and Hayley was amazed by how quickly the barn started taking shape. She heard many stories about this experience and how the Amish are able to build an entire barn in one day, but she had never seen it with her own eyes. Duncan was at the front line of everything. He did the planning and the design, his skill as a builder came in handy and it appeared that young to old admired him, but not nearly as much as she did.

When she first decided to come to Ethridge, finding love was the last thing she anticipated. After her failed engagement to Jase, she had sworn off on ever dating again, but here she was, utterly captivated by Duncan. He was the complete opposite to Jase. He was kind, considerate, a true gentleman and there was something about him that she craved.

"He's a fine young man," her gran said as she handed her the basket of fresh fruit.

Hayley tore her eyes away from the barn and smiled at her gran, "Yes, he is," she admitted.

"You know, Hannah never told us about you until after she gave you up for adoption," her grandmother started, "When she told us your grandfather begged her to withdraw the adoption and rather send you to us."

Hayley sat down opposite her gran at the wooden table, "So you did know about me?"

"Oh yes we did, but your mother had already handed you to your new parents, and we had no way of finding you. That day you arrived here in Ethridge, you were a splitting image of my Hannah."

Hayley's eyes shot full of tears and she reached out to take her grandmother's hand, "My adopted parents were good people, they really looked after me as if I was their own."

"I know, but I can't help wonder just how things would have been if Hannah had come back home," the older woman admitted and lowered her eyes.

"I'm here now though, and you've made me feel at home."

"Yah, yah, I know. I've been trying my best. Your grandfather blames himself for what happened, but he's a good man."

Hayley smiled and then looked back at the men toiling in the sun. Her grandfather was a proud but humble man, and she knew that deep down he cared for her.

By six o'clock that evening, the barn stood tall in all its glory. Brand spanking new as if no disaster had struck it just a week ago, and everyone in the community had gathered to celebrate the event. It was a festive atmosphere to say the least, and for the first time in her life Hayley felt as if she belonged. Over the weeks she spent here in Ethridge learning to bake and quilt, she hardly thought of her life in the city. And the hustle and bustle of peak hour traffic and busy shopping malls was nothing but a distant memory of a temporary life she once knew.

She made a few friends and even the older people had started to like her. Maybe it was due to the fact that she did not come here to dispute their faith or their ways, but she embraced it like any Amish citizen would.

From across the group of people she caught Duncan looking at her, but instead of looking away, she smiled at him, and even when one of his friends tapped him on his shoulder he still looked her way, refusing to drop his glance. She noticed immediately that he no longer had a beard, but that he had shaven, and the sight of him made her knees weak. It was she who first looked away when her grandfather came to sit beside her.

"My dear," he started sounding uncomfortable, "I owe you an apology for my behaviour."

Hayley turned to her grandfather and smiled, "No need, you had a lot to cope with, with my untimely arrival. I should have taken better care to notify you before I just dropped in."

"No, it's not that. I-I never gave your mother a chance to rectify things and for that I am forever guilty, I should have gone to find her."

Fredrick pinched the bridge of his nose and shut his eyes and Hayley knew he was fighting back the tears, she gently placed her hand on his, "The choices we make are our own, and we are all responsible for them, no one can take responsibility for the mistakes of others."

There was a moment of silence, and when her grandfather looked up at her again he smiled tenderly, "You will make a wonderful Amish woman," he said and patted her hand, "And Duncan would choose well to ask for your hand."

"Hayley, come!" One of the girls called and tugged her up by her hand, "You must join in on the sing."

Before Hayley could process the words of her grandfather she was caught smack bang in the middle with a bunch of the younger people, and although there were no instruments, the clapping of hands and the harmonies of voices made the songs come to life. Among the crowd was Duncan, subtly making his way closer to her and the closer he came the more her heart beat out of control and the butterflies that hijacked her insides fluttered up a storm. She might very well be an outsider but she could not deny the fact that somehow providence had claimed a victory.

"Would you spare me a few minutes of your time?" Duncan whispered as he reached her.

"Of course," she said and followed him outside.

Duncan had his hands tucked in his pockets as he stood outside. The moonlight spilled down from the heavens like a silver curtain, bathing their surroundings in silver dust and casting its subtle glow over them. And as Hayley came to stand next to him, they both glanced up into the sky.

"Hayley…"

"Duncan…"

They started at the same time and then burst out laughing.

"You first," Hayley insisted and Duncan smiled and turned towards her.

"Okay, well, I'm sure this will come as no surprise to you, but I thought it best I clear the air," he started clutching his hand in his hands, "I think or rather, I know that I have grown very fond of you, and I know that it may be a little more complicated than usual, but I have spoken to your grandfather."

Hayley stood playing with the string of her prayer cap, coiling it around her index finger nervously. It felt is if her heart was going to jump out of her throat as Duncan went on, explaining how he had asked her grandfather if he would allow him to court her. A few weeks ago, she would never have considered this, but now where she stood under the moonlit sky, with her hand in Duncan's she knew exactly what she wanted.

"And did my grandfather approve?" she asked curiously biting her lip.

"He did indeed, which is why I have gathered to courage to ask you in person," he admitted and smiled.

Hayley shifted her weight and sucked in a breath, she had no idea how Amish dating customs worked. Of all the things she had yet to learn, dating hardly featured and she recalled only briefly spot reading over that section.

"So are we going to be bundling?" she asked innocently and blushed.

Duncan raised his brows and chuckled, "My dear Hayley, you have so much to learn still, no one does that anymore," he said and stepped closer to her and reached to remove her prayer cap.

"Is that allowed?" She whispered softly as Duncan's lips hovered over hers and he pulled the pin that secured her hair in a bun lose.

"What happens between us, and the Lord, is all that matters," he said and then wrapped her lose braid around his hand and kissed her fully on the lips.

Chapter 6

Hayley stood in front of the mirror, while her grandmother fussed with her long hair. It's been a year since she joined the community and although her and Duncan's feelings for each other were no secret to the rest of the community, they both kept their word to follow the rules and customs as required by the Amish Council.

"So the food is almost ready. Once your Grandfather and I are off to the church service, you and Duncan can sit down and celebrate your betrothal."

Hayley looked in the reflection of the mirror at her grandmother, the woman she had grown to love and smiled, "Do you think I will make him happy, *Grossmammi*?" she asked.

"*Natuurlijk!* You're his future and the woman he had been waiting for all this time," her gran reassured her.

After her grandparents left to go to church, where the minister would be announcing the brides to be, she waited patiently at the house for Duncan to arrive. She kept looking at the clock on the wall, it was a unique hand crafted clock made especially for her by Duncan, as a courtship gift. Time however seemed like it had deliberately slowed down, and when she heard the carriage finally pull up in front of the house, she had to force herself to stay calm and not rush into his arms. Other than the first time he kissed her, and the second and the third, this was probably one of the most amazing moments in her life. After tonight, she would officially be engaged, and by October, only two months away, she would be Mrs. Hayley Beiler.

"You do know that you still have a choice right?" Duncan said much later, after they had finished dessert.

"I have made my choice, and it is to stay here with you," she said smiling.

They were seated on a wooden bench outside on the porch; waiting for the Lapp's to arrive.

"Are you a hundred percent sure?" he asked again, this time lacing his fingers with hers.

Hayley turned to him and placed her free hand over their entwined fingers. The past few months she had made the effort to learn their various customs, do bible study, get familiar with their laws, but she knew beyond anything that her life was here with him.

"Duncan, I am happy and I would not change this for anything," she said and then leaned close enough for her lips to brush his, "*Ich liebe dich,*" she whispered and gave him a chaste kiss on his lips.

"And I love you, Hayley Jones," Duncan said, smiling from ear to ear and then quoted Songs of Solomon, "You are altogether beautiful, my darling, beautiful in every way."

~*~

Most of all, let love guide your way. Col 3:14

The Wedding Dress

Chapter 1

Gabriela stared at her bank account, willing it to change. There was no way she was down to a hundred and twenty dollars. She wasn't getting paid for another three days! Even when she did get paid, a majority of it would get eaten up by her rent and groceries for that week. "Oh no," Gabriela said, laying her head on her arms. She didn't want to think about it, or look at it, or have anything to do with it. Unfortunately, when the problems are in your own life, you cannot exactly run away from them.

Gabriela wanted to call Bryan and get his support. She knew he would have all the verbal support she could want, but he wouldn't be able to loan her any money. His financial situation was just as bad as hers and he made even less money than she did. Once again, Gabby re-evaluated the idea of moving in with Bryan already. It would save them a few hundred bucks a month, and it wasn't so bad. After all, everyone was doing it.

"Maybe then, I would actually have money for a wedding dress," Gabby muttered to herself.

"Having a conversation with yourself again?" Reese asked her.

Gabby quickly minimized her bank account window. "Yes," she replied, trying to put aside her doubts to talk to her sister.

"You're starting to worry me. Turn that frown upside down!" Reese said, coming over and hugging Gabby.

Gabby couldn't help shaking her head and allowing a small smile to form on her lips. "Thanks, Reese." Reese started playing with Gabby's hair, brushing her fingers through its strands. Gabby closed her eyes and sunk into the sensation. It felt so calming to have her sister play with her hair as she had done since she was a little girl.

"Your graduation is in two weeks, isn't it?" Gabby asked, making slow conversation. Reese's hands felt so good.

"Yup! I can't believe I'm actually going to be done with high school. Then, I'm going to college, and that scholarship is seriously a blessing, don't you think?"

Gabby did her best at a nod. "Yes, I don't know how we would do it without that scholarship."

"Do you think Mom and Dad will come to my graduation?" Reese asked in a quiet voice. Gabby was glad she didn't have to look her sister full in the face as she answered.

"I don't know, Reese. Dad might not come because he thinks Mom will be there. Besides, he hasn't really been here for a while. I don't know. Mom might come."

"Do you think she'll bring her terrible boyfriend?"

"I don't know, Reese, but I want you to focus on your success, not on other people. You and only you have been the one responsible for getting yourself through high school. You have studied hard, and this is your time for a reward. I was thinking just you and me could go get ice cream at Scream

Cream, maybe not that night but maybe the next if you are too busy partying."

Reese knew that Gabby's money situation was tight, but she just didn't know how tight. Gabby didn't dare let Reese in on the secret. They just needed to get through the summer then Reese would be in college, and Gabby would somehow pull together enough money for just a small wedding.

"When are you going to go dress shopping?" Reese asked after a few moments of silence.

"I don't know, Reese. I will be going soon. Don't worry. You will be invited."

"Yay! You know I am so excited for you! I'll still be able to come home for Thanksgiving or fall break to wherever you guys are, right?"

"Of course, Reese!" Gabby said, finally turning and looking her sister in the eye. "Come here." Even though Reese was eighteen, Gabby was still her big sister at twenty-five. "You will always be my baby," Gabby said, trying to make Reese sit on her lap.

"No!" Reese wailed. "I shall not! I am too old to be sitting on anyone's lap."

"Mmhmm," Gabby smiled mischievously. "I'll just tell that to your striking college boyfriend when you get him."

"Eww!" Reese said. "I'm not going to sit on anyone's lap."

Gabby laughed. "Sure, you say that now. Shall I videotape you saying it and show to you in five years? Come on, help me finish making that garlic bread."

Two days later, Gabby decided to pay a visit to Bryan. They wanted to have their wedding in the middle of August. At this point, they hadn't done anything more than decide it would be held on Bryan's family farm. That decision was based on the fact that it would be a free venue, including free flowers.

"Hey, Baby," Bryan said when Gabby dropped by at dinnertime. "I made something healthy for once. You should be proud of me."

Gabby laughed. "Of course, I'm proud of you. Reese and I rebelliously did not make a salad with our meal last night, so you are doing better than me."

"Come here," Bryan said, pulling her close. He gave her a sweet kiss. When he pulled back, Gabby smiled. This was why she was with him. He always made her feel at home. "Go ahead and sit down. I'll get you a drink in a minute," Bryan commanded.

Gabby took a seat and watched Bryan careen around the kitchen, pouring drinks, draining whole wheat pasta, and preparing their plates. When they finally sat down, Gabby took his hand and listened to Bryan pray. "Thank you, God, for this meal you have given us the resources to have. Please keep giving us all that we need. Amen."

The two began eating, and Gabby finally got up the nerve to bring up the old wedding topic. "Do you think we will even be ready to get married in August? That's only two and a half months away. I'm just worried that we won't have everything ready."

Bryan sighed, but Gabby knew that his frustration was not aimed at her. "I know it's stressful. But, we've almost gotten the rings paid for." Gabby realized at that moment that she forgotten to bring her ring payment that evening.

"Sorry!" Gabby interrupted. "I forgot my payment tonight. I'm getting paid tomorrow, though. I can just give you the money then, right?"

Bryan nodded. "That's fine. I know you're tight too. But, look, we'll have a beautiful meadow, rings, our pastor will come, and gorgeous wildflowers. Maybe we can ask guests to bring a dish. I know it's not conventional," Bryan said in response to Gabby's strange look. "But, maybe they will understand. Feeding so many people can be a few thousand dollars."

"I know," Gabby nodded. "And you paint a beautiful picture. I like the way it sounds. The problem is that. . .I really want to wear a special dress. I've always dreamed of a gorgeous white wedding dress, and I just don't know if I will be able to afford one. I don't want our wedding to just pass by like it's not anything special. I want to look beautiful for you." Gabby's voice cracked with emotion, and she looked down to avoid crying.

Bryan reached over and pat her hand. "I know that it is important to you. It's important to me that you have the wedding just how you want it. But I want you to know that whatever you choose to wear, I will love it." That was when Gabby realized that her yearning to wear such a beautiful gown might not be because she wanted Bryan to think she was beautiful. Maybe she just wanted to feel beautiful for once, not for anyone else but for herself.

Chapter 2

On Saturday, Gabby left Reese sleeping at home in bed to peruse the local flea market. She needed to get Reese a graduation present, but she also didn't have a lot of money to spend on something like that. She had no idea what she wanted to get her sister, but she knew that she liked to read. Perhaps, Gabby could find a few books at a reasonable price.

Gabby was looking at a table of books, holding a couple in her hands. The three books were only twelve dollars altogether, and Gabby thought they would be a great present for Reese right before her last free summer. Gabby looked up, and her eyes fell on a shining white dress hanging on a mannequin the next stall over. Gabby left the three books on the table and walked toward the dress as if in a trance.

Her hand reached up to stroke the fabric. Just as her fingers were going to touch the fabric, Gabby wondered if she should. She looked around to see if anyone was watching her. She saw a small, elderly woman with her eyes trained on her.

"Oh, sorry," Gabby said, stumbling into an apology. "I'm sorry. I didn't know if it was alright to touch, but it's so.. .pretty."

"Go ahead," the woman said in a raspy but friendly voice. "You may touch it." Her smile encouraged Gabby just the bit she needed to have the courage. She turned back to the dress and stroked it. It was soft, almost like silk. The beadwork was amazing, with little detail stitched along the folds of the fabric. The bosom was covered with exquisite beadwork, and the waist came in before flowing out in a long skirt. The train was not overwhelming but still had a presence. It was as though someone had created a wedding gown out of Gabby's imagination.

Gabby's breath caught in her throat. She didn't want to turn away from the beauty. She stealthily scanned the dress for a price tag. Of course, there was not one. That must mean that the dress was handmade and would cost even more.

"Th-thank you," Gabby said, turning away from the dress and nodding to the woman. She took a backward step away from the dress and the woman.

"Are you getting married?" the woman asked, leaning forward encouragingly.

"Yes," Gabby nodded. "But, we don't have a date yet. It will still be a few months." Finally, she shrugged her shoulders and figured she might as well ask how much the dress cost. If she didn't, she would constantly wonder. At least with a number, she could walk away from it without feeling guilty. "How much is the dress?" Gabby nodded toward the wedding dress she had been studying.

The old woman smiled and leaned back. "Oh, that dress doesn't have a price. I'm sure you noticed. It is a beautiful and priceless piece. But," the woman continued speaking before Gabby could turn away. "I will let you wear the gown for free if you promise me one thing."

"What?" Gabby whispered, unable to wait to hear her words.

"You must live out your marriage according to God's will."

"I-uh-oh," Gabby seemed unwilling to respond. "I can wear it. . .for free?"

The woman nodded. "There's a veil that goes with the dress as well, but I must have you promise that your marriage will be uplifting to God. Can you do that?"

"I promise with my whole heart," Gabby said. She couldn't control the smile that spread across her face.

The woman nodded. "Very well. God, our good Lord, will hold you to your word. Now, just give me a moment to gather the dress and package it safely. Do you have a few minutes?"

"Yes, of course!" Gabby could hardly believe her good fortune. "Do you need any help? I could help you."

"That blue bag up there on the shelf, yes, that one. That's the veil. Go ahead and get that down, will you?" Gabby strained up to reach the high shelf, took down the bag, and could not help peering into the bag to examine the veil.

"What do you think?" the woman asked, nodding at the veil.

"It's amazing," Gabby said. The woman carefully took out the veil and used the comb part to place the veil on Gabby's head. She handed Gabby a small hand-mirror, and Gabby nearly cried. She looked like a real bride, not a bride who didn't have any money. Spontaneously, Gabby reached down and hugged the old woman. "Thank you," she sobbed out. The woman patted Gabby's back.

Finally, Gabby carefully folded the veil and put it back in the bag. She then helped the woman take the dress off the mannequin and store it in a garment bag.

"I have one more thing for you," the woman said as Gabby prepared to leave. The woman pulled out a thick book. "I want you to take a look at this. This dress, you see, has a long history. It has made many brides happy on their wedding day, and they all needed it in one way or another. I encourage you to find out about their stories and write your own as well."

Gabby took the thick, leather bound book in the crook of her arm and tried to give the woman one last hug while balancing her packages. "How will I find you again?" Gabby asked.

"I'm always right here," the woman assured her. "Come back after your wedding, and I'll be waiting."

Gabby smiled, thanked the woman one more time, then hurried out of the flea market, forgetting all about Reese's graduation present. The smile could not be wiped off her face. She carefully laid the dress across her backseat and could not help but sing along with every song on the radio. The only thing left to do was try it on. When she reached home, she carried the dress inside and explained the whole story to Reese who at first felt deceived that her sister had gone wedding dress shopping without her.

"I'm going to try it on," Gabby said. "Wait until I'm in it, okay? Don't come in!" Gabby shut the door with her sister outside and changed as carefully as she could into the wedding dress. Gabby could tell the dress had had sleeves at some point. But, it was now a sleeveless dress. The hem was a little long, but Gabby knew she could fix that. Around her waist, the dress fit perfectly. Gabby tucked the veil into place then opened the door with a smile.

"Sis!" Reese said. The smile filling her face was all that Gabby needed to see. "It's perfect isn't it?"

"Yes, it is!" Reese gave Gabby a hug. "I can't believe you are actually getting married!"

"It seems real now."

"It is real," Reese said. "I know Bryan would love you in this dress. I wish he could see it now."

"I know!" Gabby laughed. "But it has to be our secret. "No words to him about it. None, do you hear me?"

Later that night, Bryan came over. He got along well with Reese, and Gabby loved that about him. After all, she might not be Reese's official guardian, but she was Reese's home ever since their parents had started their incessant bickering.

The three were playing a game of Phase 10, and Reese kept smiling randomly at Gabby. "Is something wrong with you?" Bryan asked her. "Or do you two have a cheat going on?"

Both Gabby and Reese laughed. "Nope, we're not cheating," they said in unison.

"Okay, because that denial was totally believable. Come on, I know something is up." Gabby looked at Reese. They both shrugged, but Gabby could not longer keep the news in.

"I got my wedding dress today," Gabby said.

"What?! That's amazing, Gabby. Where is it? Can I see it? Was it expensive?"

"To all of those questions, the answer is no. Besides, the groom is never supposed to see the dress before the wedding day."

"I've got an idea," Bryan said, leaning forward. "Want to get married tomorrow?"

"Sorry," Gabby shook her head. "Pastor is occupied tomorrow. Besides, I'm not ready yet."

"Aw," Bryan visibly drooped. "I guess we should probably wait until we have rings, huh?"

"That would be important!" Gabby said. She gave Bryan a playful kiss and was glad that she did not feel as desperate for a dress as she had that morning.

Chapter 3

Gabby carefully opened the book the woman had given her the day before. In the excitement of trying on the dress and spending time with Bryan, she hadn't thought about it again until she and her sister were leaving church. She hadn't told her sister about the book or how exactly she had gotten the dress, but she had told her enough to be satisfied.

The book appeared to be some sort of journal. On the pages were handwritten notes, some in cursive, some printed, and clearly not all done by the same person. Beside each handwritten note was a picture of a woman wearing the wedding dress. Gabby ran her hands over the first picture. The dress had had sleeves, just as Gabby suspected. The picture looked old, and it was worn around the edges. But it had stayed faithfully in the book. Beside it was a note.

"Teresa Daniels, age twenty-four. Married to Bertram Frantz, age twenty-four, on May 7, 1978. My parents had both died when I was five. I had been living with a family friend since then. The boy I grew up living next to asked me to marry him, but I didn't have any money for a wedding, let alone a beautiful dress. I met this wonderful young woman who loaned me a dress that she had just finished making. She told me to tell my story and live my marriage in a way that would make God pleased with me. I am determined to do just that. My adoptive parents may not have enough money to pay for a wedding, but this wedding dress shows just how much God is looking out for us."

Underneath the note was Teresa Frantz's contact information. In different handwriting was a little note that said she had died in a car accident in 2004. Gabby suddenly felt as though she was holding something very sacred. The dress was only used perhaps once a year, if that, and Gabby hungrily read through each story. Each woman had something to say about how she did not have enough money or something had befallen her. Gabby wondered why their contact information was there. Did they really want someone to talk to them? And what did they want to talk about?

Gabby pictured herself eight years from now with a few small children. She would always remember how she had gotten her wedding dress. What would she say to someone else who was going to use it? Gabby could only smile.

She selected two of the most recent weddings and decided to write to their email addresses. Her message was simple.

"Hi, my name is Gabriela. I'm going to use the wedding dress. I found your information in the book, and I was wondering if you'd like to meet and have a coffee."

Gabriela went to bed at close to two in the morning. "I am so not going to be awake for work in the morning," Gabby said. She had received her payment in her account over the weekend, and Gabby spent a little time that Monday morning paying her bills. It was just as nasty as ever. Even though she had a wedding dress now, she still would not be able to save any money after paying everything necessary. She sighed and shook her head. "It's okay," she told herself.

The workday passed well enough, but Reese was celebrating when she got home because she only had two more exams before she was officially done with school. Gabby spent some of the evening quizzing Reese before she gave herself the luxury of checking her email. She had received a reply.

"It's nice to hear from you, Gabriela. I would love to meet for coffee. How does Wednesday at lunch hour sound? Would it be possible for me to meet you at the Starbucks in Clayton?

Annabel"

Gabriela rejoiced over the email. She couldn't wait to meet this woman and unravel a bit more of the dress mystery.

When it finally came time for her Wednesday lunch hour, Gabby drove as quickly as she could to the Starbucks. She ordered and looked around for Annabel. She finally found her, and the two shook hands in a formal manner.

"I'm so glad you reached out and contacted me," Annabel said. "I wondered if anyone ever would."

Gabby smiled excitedly. "I can't believe the dress was first loaned out in 1978. It still looks so new."

"Well," Annabel surmised. "The sleeves were taken off, and I think some extra beadwork was added."

"Still," Gabby smiled. "It's like I'm wearing a little bit of history."

Annabel laughed. "Yeah, it's magical the way that woman wants to help us. It's like she can just sense the desperation in someone."

"So, what's your story?" Gabby asked, wanting to fill in the blanks Annabel's note had left.

Annabel nodded. "I was eighteen when I got the wedding dress. I know, I was young. I didn't want to get married yet, but my boyfriend had gotten me pregnant. I had just found out a few days before. I had talked to my boyfriend, and he and I decided we would just have a quiet wedding, a justice of the peace deal. I didn't want to do that, but I knew we needed to do something quickly. I didn't want to be one of those boldly pregnant brides. But I was so frustrated with the whole situation, that I had just decided I would wear an old dress. It didn't matter.

"When I saw that wedding dress, though, I couldn't help but be drawn to it. When the woman told me it was free for my use as long as I lived a godly marriage, I couldn't believe my good fortune. We had a justice of the peace wedding, but I was wearing a gorgeously beautiful wedding gown. I will never forget that woman's generosity." Annabel shook her head.

"So, it made your day magical?" Gabriela asked in excitement.

Annabel laughed aloud. "Yes, it sure did. My wedding may not have been what I had imagined it to be when I was fifteen or sixteen, but it was much better than it would have been under the circumstances. Now, I have Gracen, and she's getting close to her second birthday."

"Wow! That's so amazing."

"What's your story?" Annabel leaned forward and listened as Gabriela told her about her all the financial troubles she had had. Gabriela and Annabel continued chatting until the last possible minute.

"I really need to get back to my job," Gabby said, "Or I could lose it. That is definitely not what I need right now. Look, I really enjoyed talking to you. Maybe we could get together again, and I could meet Gracen?"

"I'd like that," Annabel said. "I'll talk to you later."

Chapter 4

Gabriela finally got a reply from the other woman she had contacted about meeting: Brianne. Brianne's story had seemed really tragic, and Gabriela couldn't wait to hear about it from the woman's lips.

After the introductions, Gabriela leaned forward for Brianne's story. "I'm really glad you wanted to talk," Brianne said. "I feel like this dress has created a secret group."

"Have you ever talked to Annabel?" Gabriela asked.

"Annabel. . .Annabel. I don't think so. Was she married after me?"

"I don't remember," Gabriela said. "But I have her number. Maybe we could all three get together or even more brides."

Brianne smiled. "I like the idea. I am definitely willing to contribute. Okay, so here's what happened to me. My problem was not so much a financial one as I read in so many stories. Instead, my problem was a big fire. About five days before the date our wedding was set, some sort of electrical malfunction sparked in our house. My family lost everything. Insurance took care of the problem financially, but the dress I had so carefully picked out months before along with my shoes and veil had been consumed by the fire. Trying to get a dress five days before a wedding is pretty much impossible.

"But, this beautiful old lady performed a miracle. She let me borrow the dress. It was much better than the dress I had originally picked. Better than that, it was ready for the wedding two days early." Brianne shook her head. "I had thought I might need to call off the wedding. I was freaking out. I couldn't even go to work I was so stressed out. I had a few burn marks from escaping the house, but the dress covered them nicely. They can't even be seen in the photos."

"Wow!" Gabby said, soaking in her new friend's story. "Wow." She was silent for a few minutes as Brianne's story sunk in. "Did you know that there have been thirty-three weddings in that dress? I'll be number thirty-four."

"When is your wedding?" Brianne asked.

"It'll be mid-August, right after my sister moves into her college dorm. She's been living with me."

"Would you mind if I rudely invited myself to your wedding?" Brianne smiled.

Gabby laughed. "Of course not. You are welcome. It's going to be a small wedding, and we ask that each guest bring a dish of food, a sort of potluck. We really don't have the money for much more, but I would be honored for you to come."

After meeting the two brides, Gabby wanted to meet more. She kept setting up even more appointments with brides. She had one last meeting planned before her wedding. This meeting took a few weeks to set up. By the time Gabby met her, it was the first day of August.

"What's your story?" Gabby asked impatiently. The question had become one of which she could not wait to ask each new woman. Hallie had been married almost ten years ago.

"My story's probably a bit different from some others," Hallie shook her head. Gabby had agreed to come to her house because Hallie had three young children. Hallie wanted them to be able to play and stay out of their hair while the two women talked. "I was poor. I couldn't buy a wedding dress. That much is as normal as for any of us women."

Gabby nodded, anticipating more.

"My story becomes interesting after I married Mark. Did the lady have you make a promise?"

Gabby nodded. "Yes, I promised that I would live my marriage according to God's will."

Hallie accepted Gabby's words. "Yes, I promised the same thing. At the time, I promised it because it seemed such an easy exchange for the dress. But it wasn't as easy as I thought it would be. The first year of marriage was so difficult. I looked back on the innocence I sported on my wedding day, and I would shake my head. How had I thought I loved Mark?" Hallie was quiet as she remembered. "I was sure that we were going to get a divorce. You see, his family lives on the other side of the country. I know he was really close to them, but he agreed that living here would be the best solution for us.

"But, it was like he had forgotten that. We argued almost every night. I started to hate him. He made me cry so much." Hallie shook her head, and Gabby should see the tears brimming in her eyes. "I started fantasizing about running away and going a place where he wouldn't find me. Then, I remembered my promise. I tried to weasel my way out of it, saying that the fighting was Mark's fault. I blamed him, but I knew I needed to take credit for my part. So, I started serving Mark instead of myself.

"Even when I was tired, I would make dinner. I would clean up without complaint. He noticed after a month, and I felt him become more tender toward me. We were finally able to talk through what had been happening. That was the best day of my life, the day that we finally talked it all through without screaming. I finally slept next to him and felt connected to him again.

"Gabby, that promise is going to be hard to keep. You will probably get angry with your fiance sometimes, but don't walk away. The weak walk away; it's the strong that keep fighting."

Gabby hugged Hallie as a few tears spilled over. "Thank you, Hallie. I needed to hear those words. They were just what I needed." Before Gabby left Hallie's house, she invited her to her wedding. "I know it is only two weeks, but if you think you can come, I would really like it. Don't be shy about bringing your husband and children."

Chapter 5

On the day of her wedding, Gabby carefully donned the dress. It was to be a simple ceremony. Only her sister would stand beside her. Bryan was having his best friend stand beside him. At that moment nothing felt simple about Gabby as she waited for Reese to calmly do up the back.

"I can't believe it's really the day," Gabby said.

Reese smiled. "Yeah, I'm pretty sure I'm having the most exciting first weekend home from college out of all of my friends." Of course, her statement made Gabby start asking about all of Reese's new friends. She had to make sure that her baby sister was doing well and having fun in college.

"Is it done?" Gabby asked.

Reese nodded. "It's done. You're all ready."

"Well, not completely," Gabby said. "I look fine, but I feel a bit nervous about walking down that aisle."

"Why?" Reese asked. "Are you unsure about Bryan?"

"No," Gabby shook her head. "I know he is perfect for me, well, as perfect a fit as someone can be with my rather strange personality."

Reese laughed. "Then, what is making you nervous?"

"I guess it just hit me that this is a lifelong commitment. I love Bryan, and I just don't want anything to go wrong. What if we start living together, and he does annoying things that get on my nerves?"

"Like what?"

"Like leave his socks on the bed."

"Then tell him to take his socks off," Reese shrugged. "It's not that hard. Look, if you love him and you know that for sure, then you just have to go through the bad stuff and remember that. Then you'll get to the good times, and it'll be all worth it."

"Alright, my sister the wise," Gabby smiled. "What time is it?"

Reese looked at her phone. "We still have thirty minutes."

"What a long thirty minutes that'll be!" Gabby sighed, carefully sitting in her dress.

Reese laughed aloud. "I thought you just said you were nervous to do it, and now you can't wait to go down the aisle."

Gabriela laughed with her sister. "When you get to this point, I will be right by your side and remind you of everything you just said. Meanwhile, you'll just be like. No, I'm nervous! Let me be nervous by myself!"

Gabriela's friend Erica burst into the bedroom just then. "Hey! Wow, Gabby! You look so amazing!" Erica was the unofficial photographer. She had a professional camera and had done some photo shoots. A free photographer was her wedding gift to her friend. "Look, we don't have a lot of time, but I wanted to get a few pictures of just you in all your bridal beauty, then maybe a few with Reese. Hey, Reese! How are you?" Erica said in one breath.

Gabby laughed. "Oh, Erica, I knew there was a good reason we were friends." Erica took all the photos she wanted with Gabby sitting, standing, lounging, smiling, and serious.

"Alright, Reese, get in there with your sister." After a few more shots, Erica hovered over to the door. "Alright, I believe we have five minutes before your little flower girl will start her march. Let's get you safely down these stairs."

Gabby carefully maneuvered the stairs with the help of her sister and friend. The stairs were not very wide and definitely not prepared to have brides tramping up and down them. She finally stood by the back doors.

"Ready?" Reese asked.

Because Gabby had decided against having their estranged father walking her down the aisle, Reese would be walking right beside her.

"I think so," Gabby answered. "But ask me again in a minute, and I might have a different answer."

"You've got this, Sis."

"Thanks."

Erica reappeared as the music started to assist the flower girl on her way. Next went the ringbearer. After that came Gabby and Reese. It was a simple, small wedding, just as Gabby had dreamed it. Best of all was Bryan's face when she came through the doors of the back of the farmhouse.

His smile was genuine and delighted, and Gabby looked only at him as Reese guided her steps down the aisle. When she reached the altar, she placed her hands in Bryan's, smiling into his eyes and wondering how she had ever doubted her decision to marry him.

"I love you," she whispered as the pastor was talking to them. He mouthed the words back and gave her hands a squeeze. Suddenly, the ceremony, including a candle lighting, a song sung by a friend, and a short talk from the pastor seemed all too long to Gabby. After what seemed an eternity, the words she had wanted to hear for so long pierced her thoughts.

"You may now kiss the bride."

Gabby kissed Bryan, leaning into his lips. When they pulled back, Gabby felt the magic of the moment lingering. "You're my husband," she whispered, incredulous.

"And you, my dear, are my wife." Bryan let go of one of her hands, facing the audience. The pastor announced them, and Bryan paused before they started down the aisle. "This is my wife!" he shouted, his pleasure clear as he lifted up their joined hands in victory. Gabby started laughing. Suddenly, a huge cheer rose up from the back of the rows of seats. Gabby looked over and counted five of the former brides that she had met.

"Yes, Gabriela!" They screamed together. While Gabby had not pictured her wedding as loud as a ballgame, she couldn't help laughing aloud.

Bryan carefully led her down the steps, and they entered the old farmhouse. As soon as they were inside, Bryan turned to her and kissed her passionately. "You are the most beautiful bride I have ever seen," he whispered. "And tonight, I will make you mine." Gabby trembled with anticipation, leaning in for another kiss.

A week later, Gabby carefully zipped the wedding dress into the garment bag for the last time. She took out the book and carefully glued in a photo of herself wearing the dress. She smiled at the photo then took up a pen and began writing in her best cursive beside the photo.

"Gabriela Winfox, age twenty-five. Married to Bryan Davis on August 21, 2016. This dress changed my life. Not only did it give me a chance to have the kind of wedding I would never have had on my budget, but it showed me the friendliness and generosity this kind of world doesn't see very often. It made me promise to be a more generous person and to look for opportunities to help others. I didn't have any money for a nice wedding, and my fiance and I feared we would not be able to throw a wedding. Determined to get married, because we knew it was right, I thought I would never have a wedding dress. I was wrong. Please, contact me. I would love to talk to you, and I know that the brides I met would love to talk to you as well. We are in this together."

Gabriela signed her name under her words and closed the book with a solemn thud. "Thank you, God," she said as she loaded the dress, veil, and book into the back of her car. She was on her way to the flea market.

AMBER & ABEL

MONICA MARKS

Amber and Abel
Milan, Italy

"No! No! No!" Amber cried, throwing her hands up in dismay. "How did this happen? How *could* this happen?"

The others in the hung their heads in unison, no one willing to accept the blame for the most recent catastrophe.

"Giuliana is to wear the taffeta number, Gia the silk and Corina the leather and lace. Who screwed this up? Come on, speak up. Time is money, people!"

Again, only mollified silence met the designer's question.

Amber stifled a groan, knowing that she would not get an admission from the group.

"Never mind now," she sighed. "Twenty minutes to curtain. Get the models re-dressed at once. Keep an eye on the rotation! It's simple reading! It's not that complicated!"

A chorus of "yes ma'am" filled her ears and she spun to deal with the next mishap as someone shoved a clipboard in her face.

It doesn't matter how many years I've been doing this, I have yet to see a fashion show go as planned.

It was not for lack of excruciating planning of course. Every detail had been mapped to the last second months in advance and yet inevitably, someone impetrative would call in sick or a top investor would want to bring his six grandchildren backstage. Invariably, a model vomited on the runway or a make-up artist and hair stylist got into a fist fight.

It was what kept Amber's blood pressure skyrocketing and her heart rushing in her ears.

"Amber! Amber, you have an urgent phone call!"

Her assistant, Dana appeared, holding out one of the three cell phones she carried but Amber waved her away.

Every phone call was an urgent phone call. It was an occupational hazard.

"Not now, Dana. Can't you see we're T minus nineteen minutes?"

"Amber, you need to take – "

"Dana! I am up to my ears in disasters right now. Can you please deal with whatever it is? Is that not what I pay you the big bucks for?"

For a timeless second, a hush seemed to fall over the bustling backstage and inexplicably, Amber felt the hairs on her arms raise as she lifted her head.

She looked at Dana who shook her head quietly.

"What is it?" Amber breathed. "What happened?"

Dana visibly swallowed, lowering her kind, brown eyes through the lenses of her glasses.

She extended the phone further.

"It's your mother."

And Amber's world stopped.

<u>Brooklyn, New York</u>

"I'm looking for Leah Colville," Amber told the nurse. She drummed her fingers anxiously on the counter as the woman punched in the information and nodded.

"Room 717," she announced. "Just follow that hallway to the end."

Amber barely heard the last words as she flew down toward her mother's room.

It was slightly ajar and she pushed it open, her stomach flipping nervously.

"Mama?" she called softly. "Mama, are you awake?"

"Amber?"

She hurried inside the semi-private room, sliding the separating curtain aside.

Leah was the only one in the room but Amber knew that could change at the drop of a hat.

Oh mama, why didn't you say anything?

Her breath caught in her throat as she stared at her one virile mother, sunken in the bed, her face as white as the sterile sheets in which she lay.

Amber threw herself into her mother's arms gently.

"Oh mama," she whispered. "Why didn't you tell me it had gotten so bad?"

Leah made a dismissive sound with her tongue.

"You are a busy girl, Amber. The last thing you need is your old, sick mom crying in your ear about chemo treatments and hair loss. It's nothing you haven't heard a million times before."

Tears filled Amber's grey eyes but she hid them.

"I am never too busy for you," she scolded tenderly. "How long have you been like this?"

Leah sighed.

"Three weeks. The doctors are shocked I've hung on this long, kitten. It's only a matter of time..."

A stunning bolt of guilt almost brought Amber to her knees.

How could I not have known for three weeks? What kind of daughter am I?

"Don't talk like that!" Amber cried. "You're not going to..."

She trailed off as her voice caught in her throat.

"Shh, kitten. Don't cry now. We have both known that I have been living on borrowed time for a long while. God has been gracious enough to let me see you become successful and now I can go to the other side knowing you are secure."

Amber pursed her lips together, squeezing her mom's frail body.

"But I need you to do something for me," the older Colville woman continued and Amber raised her head.

"Anything, mama. Tell me what you need."

Leah studied her beautiful daughter's face for a long moment, reaching up to stroke her short, layered hair.

"Two things actually."

Amber stared at her expectantly.

"First, when I die, I need you to go to Pennsylvania and find my sister, Ruthie to let her know I've passed."

Amber stared at her uncomprehendingly.

"Your sister Ruthie?" she echoed. "Since when do you have a sister Ruthie?"

Leah offered her a weak smile.

"I have always had a sister, kitten."

Amber waited for her to elaborate but Leah seemed to have lost her strength suddenly.

"I'm tired, Amber," she murmured. "I would like to rest now."

"Yes, mama, of course," Amber replied, sitting up. "I will be right here when you wake up."

Leah patted her daughter's hand and smiled lovingly.

"The second thing I would like you to do it grow your hair long again. I miss those golden locks of yours."

Amber forced a smile through the tears in her eyes.

"I will do that mama. I will grow my hair and find Aunt Ruthie in Pennsylvania."

Leah nodded slowly, her eyes growing heavy.

"Just Ruthie, not Aunt Ruthie. You can find her in Eden, Pennsylvania. Ruthie Miller."

Amber watched with a trembling chin as her mother's eyes fell closed knowing that it was the last time she would ever see them open again.

Eden, Pennsylvania

Amber looked at the woman embarrassed.

"I'm afraid I don't know much more than what I've already told you," Amber admitted, wishing away the clerk's scornful scrutiny. "My mother asked me to find her sister here in Eden and I have no idea where to start."

The clerk gave her a look which was half bemused, half annoyed but she turned back to her computer.

"Ruth Miller," she sighed, shaking her head. "There has to be at least two dozen here and that's only the ones we have one record."

Amber blinked and stared at her.

"This is city hall, isn't it? Why wouldn't you have them on record? Do you have a lot of illegal immigrants here?"

Amber's question was sincere but the clerk's expression turned sardonic.

"You really are not from around here, are you?"

Amber swallowed her annoyance and forced a smile.

"No, ma'am. I am not. That is why any help you can give me would be greatly appreciated. Why would you not have someone on record?"

"This is Amish country, honey."

Amber suddenly felt foolish and she grinned sheepishly.

"Of course. Well, can you see if any of the Ruth Millers you have there have a sister named Leah?"

The clerk's red eyebrows rose almost to her hairline.

"Ruth and Leah Miller? Are you kidding me? You're definitely looking for an Amish family, sweetie."

"That can't be," Amber said shaking her head. "My mom wasn't Amish."

"Well, I can check but if it quacks like a duck..."

Again, her fingers flew over the keyboard and she raised an eyebrow.

"I have two Ruth Millers with a sibling named Leah."

She scrawled their telephone numbers onto a piece of paper for her.

"But I wouldn't get your hopes up, honey," the clerk told her as she held out the sheet. "My guess is that your Ruth Miller is somewhere in the countryside."

Amber stared at her helplessly.

"What do I do then?"

"If neither of these women is who you're seeking, I would start combing the districts."

Amber opened her mouth to ask what that meant but the older woman seemed irritated enough.

She closed her mouth and vowed to find someone else to help her find answers.

Instead, she thanked her and hurried out of the building, into the windy autumn day.

As she stood on the steps, looking down at the phone numbers in her hands, a memory flittered through her mind.

She had been about four years old and her mother pulled a long dress from a hope chest at the foot of the bed.

It had been just after Amber's father had died and Leah had been so melancholic, digging through old photos and keepsakes.

"That's an old dress, mama," Amber said, looking at the homespun fabric in awe.

"It is, kitten, yes," her mother agreed. "Would you like to try it on?"

"Yes please!" Amber cried and Leah had laughed, slipping the too large garment onto her small daughter.

The older Colville dug into the chest and removed a small white cap, placing it on the base of Amber's head.

"You look like a proper Amish girl now, *Liebchen*."

"What is an Amish girl, mama?"

"Greta!"

The voice was loud and almost directly in her ear, smashing her reverie into a million pieces.

Startled, Amber turned to look.

An Amish man stood behind her, his green eyes alight with hope as she met his stare.

"Greta, you've returned!" he said excitedly. "When did you come back to Eden?"

Amber shook her head.

"I'm sorry," she said kindly, still awed by the green of his irises. "You have me confused with someone else."

To her surprise, his brow furrowed and he scowled slightly.

"Are you playing a game?" he asked gruffly, his eyes narrowing. "You don't need to worry; I won't tell anyone I have seen you."

Amber's eyes widened and she wondered if she was in the middle of a gag.

She looked around for cameras but nothing seemed out of the ordinary.

"I really am sorry," she said again, continuing down the steps. "You have me mixed up with someone else. My name isn't Greta."

She hurried away before he could respond, leaving him staring after her.

As she made her way toward the street where her rental car waited, she glanced back uneasily at the attractive man, her heart racing.

That was strange, she thought, sliding into the driver's side.

But as she pulled away from the curb, she wondered if it was less strange and more fate.

Perhaps that man was God's way of telling her that she would find her long lost aunt inside the Amish community after all.

I guess it's time to start combing the districts, Amber thought wryly. *Whatever that means.*

She could not help but take one last peek at the man in her rear-view as she drove away. He remained standing on the steps, staring after her as if he expected her to return.

I hope he finds Greta, she thought wistfully. *He certainly seems to love her.*

"Abel, who was that?" Levi demanded, rushing up the steps of city hall to meet his brother. He peered in the direction which the car gone.

"Apparently no one," Abel muttered as he watched the small sports car zoom away from the center of town.

"From where I stood, it looked to be Greta Shetler and – "

"It was not," Abel snapped, cutting off his brother before another word could leave his lips.

Levi eyed him warily.

"You seem upset," he commented. "Hasn't that woman done enough damage to you without having you pine for her?"

"Let's not speak about her," Abel said between clenched teeth as he hurried down the steps. "We have errands to run."

Levi chuckled dryly.

"Well whoever she is, I would not mind seeing her again," Levi commented. Abel paused to give his brother a scathing look.

"She is an Englisher," he retorted. "You would do well to stay away from her."

"Why? Are you interested?" Levi mocked. "And I thought you were going to die longing for the shunned and shamed beauty of the district."

"You are speaking nonsense now, Levi," Abel chided. "If you can't speak normally, don't speak at all."

Abel didn't have to look over to know his brother was leering at him.

It seemed everyone in town had been ogling him since the day Greta had run off with the Englisher, leaving him at the altar after declaring she was pregnant with the Englisher's child.

And now she was back, pretending that she did not recognize him.

It was just another slap in the face after her ex-communication, almost two years earlier.

Has she come back to humiliate me further?

"Who was she if not Greta?" Levi demanded, obviously unwilling to leave the topic alone.

"You know you should not even be speaking her name," Abel snapped. "I don't know who that woman was."

"Then why did you run after her if you don't know her?"

Abel was growing angry with his brother's interrogation.

"Let us go our own way today. We can accomplish more that way."

Without permitting Levi an opportunity to answer, he rushed away, trying to leave his brother in his wake along with the painful memories of Greta.

After finding a quiet spot to park her car, Amber picked up her cell phone.

She tried both the phone numbers given to her by the clerk at city hall but as the woman had predicted, neither was the woman Amber sought.

Now I have to venture from district to district, she realized. She was not looking forward to the task; it seemed daunting but she knew she could not rest until she had honored her mother's wishes.

Instinctively, she reached up and touched her hair.

It had already begun to grow out some in the two months since Leah's passing and Amber was determined not to touch it.

As she drove the rental into the outskirts of Eden, the lush Pennsylvania hills fell into a smaller settlement of land and soon, she could see that she was inside the Amish district.

Almost immediately, a feeling of peace overcame her and she had to stop the car to admire the almost surreal beauty of the landscape around her.

She grabbed for her cell phone, snapping pictures as the horizon as the sun began to set over the lolling dales.

Suddenly, she heard the clopping of hooves as a wagon approached and Amber lowered her camera, watching in awe as a horse and cart ambled toward her.

In the front, a man and woman dressed in traditional Amish attire rode primly and Amber offered them a nervous smile, not knowing if she would be received with distain.

To her relief, they both returned her beam and the man slowed the beast.

"Are you lost, miss?" he asked politely and Amber shook her head.

"No…well maybe," she replied sheepishly. "I stopped to take a picture of the beautiful landscape but…"

She trailed off, suddenly embarrassed.

"I am afraid I'm on a bit of a wild goose chase," she confessed. They peered at her with curious eyes.

"Are you looking for someone's home?" the woman asked. "Perhaps we can direct you."

Amber opened her mouth to answer and then closed it.

"This is going to seem ridiculous," she muttered. "But I am looking for a woman named Ruthie Miller. Do you know her?"

The couple seemed slightly amused by the question and Amber was beginning to realize that was going to be a common response to her inquiry.

I wonder what it would be like to live in a place where everyone knew everyone else? I imagine there is a sense of security that accompanies that knowledge.

"I fear that we know several women by that name, miss. Can you tell us anything else about her?"

"She had a sister named Leah but they have been estranged for – "

Suddenly, Amber found it difficult to speak and she swallowed quickly as her voice broke.

"Have you had supper, miss?" the woman asked quietly. "Our farm is not far from here. It would be our pleasure to have you as our guest."

Amber looked up, terrified and shook her head.

"Oh no, I couldn't," she gulped. "But thank you."

The man smiled.

"It is considered very rude to refuse a supper invitation in Amish country," he informed her and Amber could see he was teasing her but all the same, she found herself nodding.

"That would be lovely," she breathed. "Thank you."

"You may follow us," the woman said, smiling.

Amber nodded and allowed them to pass before jumping back into her car.

What lovely people, she thought, her heart warming. The man on the steps of city hall had made her nervous and so far, he had been the only interaction she had with anyone in their culture.

But he did have lovely green eyes.

Amber steered the Chrysler into up the long drive of the pretty farmhouse, keeping a safe distance behind the kind strangers.

Slowly, she exited her car, suddenly aware of how strange was what she was doing.

Would I ever accept such an unexpected dinner invitation from random strangers in New York or Milan or Paris? Of course not. So why am I doing it here?

The answer was obvious; it felt right.

She was nowhere near any major city, designing clothes and fighting with stage hands or arguing with models.

It was like she had entered another world, another planet even where Amber Colville didn't exist and she was just a lost little girl, looking for the last family relation she had left in the world.

Does my Aunt Ruthie have children? Maybe I have cousins out there. Or should I say, in here.

"Come along, miss. It's growing cold without the sun shining down on us," the woman urged.

"My name is Amber," she volunteered as she was led into the house. "Amber Colville."

The wife smiled and nodded.

"That is a lovely name. I am Beth and that is my husband, Jeremiah Troyer."

"Pleased to meet you, Mr. and Mrs. Troyer," I said politely.

She smiled softly.

"We do not use such formalities here. You may call us Beth and Jeremiah," she said softly.

Amber blushed lightly and nodded.

"Only if you call me Amber," she agreed.

"Please, come and sit. Our boys should be along shortly. They have been commissioned with supper as Jeremiah and I were in town today."

"I see," she said, nodding. "But you are farmers?"

"Yes," Beth replied. "We grow wheat and barley. Our boys have recently acquired chickens but between you and I, Amber, I am rather fearful of their pecking beaks."

Amber chuckled with Jeremiah.

"There is no shame in having fears, Beth," her husband said, reassuringly. "I am certain even the English have fears."

Amber's smile broadened.

"Oh yes," she assured them. "More fears than I care to admit."

A sudden warmth flowed between them as they stood in a comfortable silence.

"Come along inside," Jeremiah said, shooing them from the foyer. "I will see about some cider. It is cooling in the shed. Abel just made a fresh batch."

"He's a good boy, our eldest," Beth murmured but Amber noticed a dark cloud cross over her eyes as if something occurred to her.

She stared at Amber, her mouth parting slightly.

"Is something wrong, Beth?" Amber asked, immediately concerned by her change of disposition.

The older woman shook her head.

"I will help Jeremiah with the cider. The barrel can be difficult to manage. Please, sit by the fire until we return."

She was gone before Amber could reply and she was abruptly filled with a small fission of alarm.

That was strange, she thought but she was ashamed of her suspicion. *Things are just done differently here than they are in the city. There's nothing strange about it.*

"*Mamm! Daed?*"

She turned her head as a man called out, poking his head into the sitting room where Amber had sunk into a wing chair.

He seemed to freeze as he looked at her.

"Hello," Amber volunteered. "I'm Amber Colville. Your parents have invited me for dinner."

A small smile appeared on the young man's lips and he stalked toward her, extending his hand.

"Levi Troyer," he announced. "You were in Eden today, were you not?"

Surprised, Amber nodded.

"Yes, I was at city hall, looking for information."

Levi's eyebrow raised.

"What sort of information?" he asked curiously, placing himself into the chair facing her.

Amber swallowed and shook her head.

"It's not really important," she said quickly. "I would rather not get into it right now."

Levi's blue eyes narrowed slightly.

"I can be a wonderful source of information," he told her. "If you ever feel like talking."

His meaning was unmistakable and Amber found herself amused and slightly intrigued by the forward speaking man.

"Thank you," she replied, laughing. "Perhaps after dinner. It's not a very cheerful supper conversation."

"Levi, why did you leave me alone to finish supper. I have – "

Amber turned toward the doorway again and her jaw dropped.

"Wh -what is she doing here?" the man gasped, looking accusingly at his brother. Levi jumped to his feet, grinning.

"It appears as thought *Mamm* and *Daed* have invited her over for supper. Amber, this is my brother, Abel."

Cautiously, Amber rose to her feet, unsure of how Abel would react to her as she recalled their previous encounter.

"Hello Abel," she said quietly. "Pleased to meet you."

She wasn't sure if she should extend her hand or not but she found herself once more staring into his impossibly green eyes as if hypnotized.

He did not immediately respond and Amber felt her heart sink slightly as he continued to stare at her.

"Forgive my brother," Levi interceded. Amber turned questioningly to him.

"He seems to think you look like someone he knew once a long time ago," Levi offered and Amber nodded slightly.

"I never said that," Abel grumbled but Amber felt that his gaze betrayed his words. He could not seem to pull his irises from her face as if trying to memorize every feature.

"There you are," Beth said, hurrying into the front room, a concerned expression on her face. She held out a glass for Amber.

"This is apple cider from the Bachman's orchid," she told Amber, smiling briefly. The older woman seemed to sense the tension in the room.

"I see you have met our sons, Abel and Levi," she continued as Amber accepted the cup. "What have you made for supper, boys? I am sure our guest is as hungry as your father."

"What did the doctor say, *Mamm*?" Abel asked suddenly, diverting his attention to his mother.

Beth's face turned pale and angry.

"Abel, that is hardly an appropriate question to ask before visitors. Go tend to supper," she snapped with a harshness Amber was sure was not customary.

Abel seemed contrite but he disappeared, bowing his head somewhat shamefully.

Amber felt a spark of apprehension in her stomach as she cast Beth a sidelong look.

Why did she go to the doctor? Is she ill? Does she have cancer like mama?

Amber bit on her lower lip and tried to push the image of her mother from her mind but it was more difficult than she wished.

"Are you all right, Amber?" Beth asked, her brow furrowing deeper as she watched the blonde's face crumble.

Amber tried to nod but a tear escaped her and slid down her cheek.

"I'm sorry," the younger woman told the others, quickly wiping the streak from her face. "I recently lost my mother and I was just thinking of her. Forgive me for my display."

Beth and Levi made a commiserating noise.

"Levi, go help your brother and leave the women to talk," Beth ordered. Levi rose without protest, leaving them alone in the front room.

"It is difficult to lose a parent," Beth said comfortingly. "I have lost both of mine."

Amber sighed.

"I am so sorry, Beth. My father also died when I was very young."

Beth leaned down to pat her hand soothingly and Amber found the gesture heartwarming.

I am a perfect stranger to her and yet she feels the need to comfort me. This place is like a television program. This isn't real life. This is a place where daughters would know that their mothers have been dying for weeks, not off running fashion shows in Italy.

"Supper is ready, *Mamm*, Amber," Levi called from the dining room and the women rose to join the others at the dinner table.

"We pray before eating, Amber. You are not required to join us," Jeremiah told her as she took a seat across from the Troyer brothers.

"I would be happy to join in your prayer if you'll have me," Amber replied. She pretended not to notice the look of appreciation shared by the family as she hung her head.

Jeremiah lead the prayer in Pennsylvania Dutch but Amber could catch some of the key words from the time she had spent in Munich.

"You still have not told us what you are doing in our district, Gre – ah, Amber," Levi piped up after they had loaded their plates with meat, vegetables, potatoes and bread.

Beth and Jeremiah looked up sharply while Abel's jaw tightened.

"Were you going to call me Greta also?" Amber asked, her eyes widening. Levi seemed embarrassed.

"You do bear an uncanny resemblance to her," he confessed.

"I did not notice," Beth interjected, eyeing her older son.

"Nor did I!" Jeremiah agreed and there was a finality in his tone. It was clear that the subject was to be dropped and Amber did not want to push the issue.

Nevertheless, she was fascinated by the fact she might have an Amish twin.

"I have come here looking for my mother's sister but I'm afraid I don't have much to go off. I don't even know if I'm looking in the right spot but my mom only told me about her before she died."

Beth looked up and smiled.

"We told Amber we would happily help her find her aunt but we would need to narrow the search somehow."

"What is her name?"

Amber was surprised it was Abel who asked the question.

"Ruthie Miller. Her sister, my mother, was Leah."

The table fell silent as the family appeared to rake their memories.

"Well, I can think of four women by that name. One is far too young to be your aunt, one is much too old and the other two have lived in the district all their lives without a sister named Leah," Jeremiah volunteered, chewing his fried steak pensively. "Have I forgotten someone?"

"No...I do not believe you have," Beth replied. She gazed at her boys.

"Any suggestions?"

Levi shrugged his shoulders.

"As Amber has said, there is no guarantee that this Ruthie Miller is from this district. Perhaps I could take her to the neighboring districts tomorrow and we could investigate further."

He beamed at her and Amber smiled back but she could not help her gaze from falling on the older Troyer brother.

He seemed to glower into his plate, unspeaking.

"That would be lovely," Amber said reluctantly, realizing that Abel was not about to volunteer his help.

Is he always so brooding or is it because I remind him of this Greta?

"It's settled then. Tomorrow I will take you in search of your aunt!" Levi said jovially.

Amber could not help but notice that he gently jabbed his brother in the ribs and she wondered if she hadn't put herself in the middle of a sibling rivalry.

Abel could not sleep and he lay on his back, arms folded across his chest.

"I can feel you breathing fire over there, Abe," Levi called mockingly through the dark. "Why are you so upset?"

"I'm not!" Abel denied but Levi only laughed.

"Why don't you just admit that you want to take Amber on her search tomorrow?"

"I do not," he replied hotly but as he said the words, he knew they were a lie.

He couldn't seem to get over the remarkable likeness Amber shared to Greta. It was as if *Gotte* had sent him a chance to get things right with Greta.

That's ridiculous. They are two different women. If Levi wishes to waste his time with an Englisher, let him do it.

"You truly are a fool," Levi sighed, sitting up. Abel turned his head to scowl at his brother in the moonlit room.

"You would know a fool to see one, brother," he snapped. "Stop talking and let me go to sleep."

Levi groaned.

"I only offered to take Amber tomorrow because I knew you wouldn't. You will pick her up at her hotel in Eden and take her."

"I will not!" Abel was insulted at the idea of stealing his brother's date. "She has agreed to go with you, not me."

"But she wants to go with you," Levi insisted. "She could not stop staring at you all through dinner. Didn't you notice?"

Abel had not.

"Of course you didn't notice. You were too busy sulking about Greta to notice the lovely woman yearning for you to look at her. I think Amber is *Gotte's* way of telling you that it is time to move on."

"What do you know?" Abel growled but in his heart, he felt a sliver of hope.

Is he just telling me that because he believes I have spent too much time pining over Greta or did Amber find me interesting?

"I know that if you don't act on this opportunity, I will give you no more second chances. I will pursue Amber myself."

Abel didn't answer but his heart sank at his brother's words.

Maybe this is a sign from Gotte. What harm can it do to take her tomorrow?

Amber felt a spark of happiness when she saw Abel at the reins the following morning in front of the Eden Resort and Suites.

"I hope you do not mind that I have come in my brother's place," Abel said, somewhat gruffly but Amber was already learning that it was shyness, not rudeness.

"I am very happy it was you," she replied earnestly, catching his eye.

A shiver coursed down her spine as he helped her onto the wagon and they made their way out of town toward the districts.

She found herself studying his handsome profile, taking in the fine shape of his nose and delicate bone structure.

"I hope that you will not be disappointed," Abel told her as they started their ride in silence.

Amber glanced at him in surprise, thinking that he had caught her staring at him.

She blushed and shook her head.

"I'm not disappointed in the least," she replied, lowering her eyes.

He shot her a sidelong look and gave her a lopsided smile.

"I meant that I hope you find your aunt," he explained. Amber turned bright red and cleared her throat in nervousness.

"Of course," she muttered, doubly ashamed.

She had almost forgotten the reason for their drive as if they were merely on a date.

Focus on the task at hand, she told herself.

Soon, they were in one of the neighboring districts and Abel proved to be a wonderful guide, finding a minister to question almost immediately.

They did not find anyone to match their description in the first two districts they visited but as they made their way into the third, it was growing late in the afternoon and Amber was growing disheartened.

"I'm beginning to think this is a lost cause," Amber confessed as they searched for the home of the deacon as directed by a young girl playing hopscotch.

Despite her mounting disappointment, she could not shake the idyllic beauty of their community.

I would give it all up to live here, she thought as they found Deacon Roth tending to his herb garden.

"Hello, Deacon," Abel called. "I am Abel Troyer and this is my friend, Amber. We have some questions for you if you have a moment."

The deacon looked up and nodded, smiling welcomingly.

"Of course," he agreed. "What can I help you with?"

"Deacon, have you a Ruthie Miller who lives here? She would be in her forties or fifties with an estranged sister named Leah?"

The elderly man's mouth parted and he stared at Amber for a long moment.

"Indeed," he murmured. "Are you Ruthie's daughter?"

Amber shook her head.

"No...I am Leah's daughter," Amber replied, glancing nervously at Abel. "Do you know them?"

The man nodded thoughtfully.

"Of course, I remember Leah. She never was baptized. She fell in love with an Englisher and married him when she was nineteen or so."

Amber nodded excitedly.

"Yes! Alexander Colville. That was my father," Amber gushed. "Is Ruthie still here?"

"No, child. Ruthie was married to a man named Samuel Miller but he died in a terrible accident not two years after the wedding. That was about a year after Leah had left the district."

Amber found her palms sweating and she wiped them on her jeans.

"Where did she go? Did my aunt leave the community too?"

The deacon chuckled.

"No, no. She eventually remarried and moved on to another district."

"Nearby?" Amber pressed, her excitement mounting.

I'm so close to finding your sister, mama! She thought, her heart racing.

"Yes, two districts across."

Abel's face turned confused.

"Closest to Eden?" he asked and the older man nodded.

"But that's our district," Abel murmured. A look of understanding crossed his face.

"Who did she marry when she moved?" he asked.

The deacon thought for a long moment, digging into the depth of his swiss cheese memory bank.

"Ah yes. David Shetler. As far as I know, they still live there but I confess, I am out of touch sometimes," Deacon Roth chortled.

Abel's face turned grey.

"Do you know these people, Abel?" Amber asked excitedly. "Do you know where I can find them?"

He looked at her, his face aghast.

"Yes," he whispered. "I know them. They are Greta's parents. You are Greta's cousin."

The ride back to Eden was long and quiet as Abel tried to gather his thoughts. To his relief, Amber did not push him to speak as if she could sense he needed the quiet.

Is this a cruel joke? Sending me a cousin of the woman who broke my heart? One who looks so much like her?

But as they continued the journey back, Abel suddenly realized that he had been blinded by Amber's outward appearance.

True, she looked like Greta with the solemn grey eyes as sunny blonde hair but how similar were the two really?

Greta could not seem to run away fast enough, sacrificing her own values to do so while Amber embraced her mother's home and heritage in tribute.

Greta was selfish and hurtful while Amber was kind and loving.

Greta was gone and Amber was right there beside him, waiting for him to speak, to make the next step.

"It is getting late," he finally told her. "I don't think it is wise to interrupt your aunt at this hour although I am certain she will be happy to see you, regardless of the time."

Amber nodded but he could see the sadness in her eyes.

"That's fine. I can find my own way there tomorrow," she replied, trying to sound cheerful. "But I appreciate all your help."

She turned her head quickly but he knew it was only so he wouldn't see the tears in her eyes.

He paused, searching for the next words to say.

Opening his mouth, his perfectly concocted statement flew into the air.

"I am hungry," he said instead.

Amber turned to glance at him.

"You're hungry?" she repeated. "Oh."

She wasn't quite sure what to make of the statement.

"Me too," she replied suddenly.

Their eyes met and they smiled.

"May I buy you dinner, Amber?" he asked her sweetly.

"Like a date?" she teased.

His smiled faded and he nodded solemnly.

"Exactly like a date," he replied.

END

LOVINA'S HEART

DEIDRA SCOTT

152

Chapter One

Lovina Miller took a deep breath as she reached up to pull a piece of laundry from the clothesline and put it in the basket at her feet. Above her head, a pair of bluebirds danced through the bright June sky, reminding her that summer was quickly approaching.

Summer. It was a time full of fresh starts and new beginnings.

Looking across the yard, Lovina watched David Yoder working with one of her brothers. Together, the two young men were struggling with their task, trying to break her *daed's* new horse.

Ach, just watching David sent a thrill of excitement through Lovina's heart. Although she had known him most of her life, there was something about him that could still put a spark inside of her, giving her the feeling that they had just met.

Growing up, Lovina had always dreamed of marrying David. It had just seemed natural to her. With their two houses located side-by-side, they had spent all of their childhood hours playing together in the creek that wound between their properties and climbing the big apple tree like little monkeys.

Lovina had decided early on that she and David would grow old together, spending their adult days raising babies and making a life within their Amish community.

Now that Lovina had turned eighteen-years-old, she felt like she was stuck in the midst of a waiting game, simply counting down the hours until David came forward to begin their relationship together.

Smiling to herself, Lovina basked in the realization that, as an adult, it was now time to watch her childhood dreams start to unfold.

"*Danki* for the help, David!" Lovina heard her father call out from the barn and looked up in time to see David waving goodbye to her family as he started across the yard.

Lovina felt her heart go aflutter when, rather than take the path back to his own parents' house, David veered closer to her own home and made a bee-line right for the clothesline where she was working.

"*Gut* afternoon, David!" Lovina called out, her voice seeming somewhat weak to her own ears.

Watching him come closer, Lovina couldn't help but marvel at how handsome her childhood friend had become. With a head-full of dark red hair and sparkling blue eyes, David had always looked like a cheerful storybook character; however, as he aged, he grew tall and muscular, his boyish looks transforming into that of a good-looking man.

"Hello there, Lovina," David called back, rolling down his sleeves as he walked along, "I tell you, that horse of your *daed's* nearly got me down this time!"

Lovina smiled as she pulled a pair of her brother's pants off of the laundry line and tossed them in the basket, "I guess we should consider ourselves glad to have such a good horse-breaker living so near-by."

To her surprise, David's face suddenly seemed to darken. Taking a deep breath, he reached up and put one hand on the clothesline, "Actually, Lovina, I wanted to talk to you about that."

Although Lovina had hoped that David would want to talk to her alone, she could already tell that his news wasn't going to be what she had wanted to hear.

"Lovina," David looked out across the fields, "Ever since you had your birthday, I'd been hoping..." his voice trailed off and he gave a shrug, "Well, nothing I'd hoped for is going to work out this summer." Standing up taller, he announced, "My uncle from Indiana wrote telling about the need for a good horse-trainer in his community. I agreed to go help for the next three months...I'll be home in time to help my dad get started on the harvest."

Lovina felt her heart drop in her chest. The idea that David would leave had never entered her mind. Even though it was only for three months, it felt like it might as well be three years.

"*Ach*, Lovina, don't be so sad," David reached out and placed his hand on her arm, "I'll be back – I promise. Kentucky is my home...I sure don't have any plans to run off for good."

Something about having his hand on her arm made the pain a little more bearable. Looking up, Lovina met David's tender gaze with her own.

"When I come back..." David took a deep breath and kicked at a clump of grass with his foot. It was strange to see him so uncomfortable – David was usually one to be bold and daring, willing to say whatever was necessary.

"When I come back, I hope we can spend more time together," David managed to say, "Seems like we've grown apart over the years, and I'm ready for that to end."

Lovina couldn't stop the smile that spread across her face, "And maybe not be climbing trees this time?" She added.

David laughed, "Of course we'll be climbing trees again!" He teased.

Growing more sober, he lifted his hand and ran it gently across her cheek, "I'll see you in three months, 'Vina."

Three months. As she watched him walk away and back to his parents' farm across the creek, Lovina took a deep breath and tried to still her thumping heart. Three months was a long time – she was just glad that she had those tender moments to cling to during the summer that stretched out before her.

Chapter Two

Taking a deep breath, David watched out the passenger window as the driver he had hired took him farther and farther from his home in Kentucky and on toward his Uncle Amos' house in Indiana.

"Are you nervous about leaving home for so long?" David's paid driver, Mr. Simpson asked, as he flipped his turn signal on and proceeded toward Uncle Amos' house.

David shook his head and laughed, "*Ach*, no, not nervous."

"Anxious to get away from your parents?" Mr. Simpson asked with a chuckle.

"No, nothing like that." David assured him, "Just glad to be helping my uncle and the people in his community."

Leaning his head back against the headrest of the seat, David closed his eyes and thought about Mr. Simpson's question.

Was he glad to be getting away from his parents? Although he had been quick to assure his driver that wasn't he case, David wasn't so certain himself. To be completely honest, David wasn't a bit sorry to be leaving for the summer. While he had always loved his home and his family, David relished the chance to get away.

Since David had been a little boy, he had always known what was expected of him. He was going to settle down, buy a piece of property close to his parents, and marry Lovina Miller. It wasn't a bad plan at all, but it seemed so boring and dull. Deep in his heart, David had always dreamed of excitement and adventure. Maybe his trip to Indiana would finally provide him with a chance to enjoy his freedom before he settled down for good.

David's driver took him straight to Uncle Amos' house, helped him unload his bags, and then left him to head back to Kentucky.

Uncle Amos and his entire family were happy to welcome David to their home. Uncle Amos explained that everyone in the community could use his horse breaking services and that they would be bringing their horses to his house so that David could train them. Uncle Amos also said that, during David's spare time he could help the family out in the dry goods store they had located in a small shed next to the road.

"I'll take you out to the store now, so that I can show you what kind of work you can do out there." Uncle Amos suggested once David had put his clothes away in the spare bedroom.

Leading David across the yard, Uncle Amos explained, "Of course, I will pay you for helping in the store...and you can also have all the money for training the horses."

David shook his head, "*Ach,* that's too much, Uncle Amos. I'm happy to have the chance to help out."

Uncle Amos chuckled and reached out to give David a slap on the back, "Now, now, don't go talking like that. I'm sure a handsome young man like you should be saving back to buy a nice farm and making plans for the future. I'd dare say that some pretty girl back home has caught your eye."

David gave a shrug, not too anxious to think about his future, "Nothing set in stone just yet."

The graveled lane ended and the two men found themselves standing side-by-side outside of the dry goods store. Reaching out, Uncle Amos pushed the door open, revealing a building with shelves full of baking supplies, canned goods, and some craft items.

"Hannah!" Uncle Amos called out, as he led David through the small building, "Hannah!"

"I'm over here," a soft voice returned.

Turning the corner around one of the shelves, they found a young Amish woman on her knees, busy stacking bags of flour.

"Hannah, I want you to meet my nephew, David," Uncle Amos announced, "David, this is Hannah – she is my wife's cousin and she's helping us out in the store this summer."

Hannah pulled herself to her feet and turned to stare up at David with large, blue eyes. Wisps of dark hair had escaped her prayer *kapp,* making a sort of halo around her face.

Just looking at her, David felt his heart give a leap. She was so unexpectedly beautiful in a dark, mysterious way.

"*Gut* to meet you, David," Hannah replied timidly.

"David is likely to be helping out in the store when he isn't working with the horses," Uncle Amos explained. Giving David a pat on the arm, he motioned toward the back room, "Come on, I want to show you where I store the bulk supplies."

As David followed his uncle, he had a hard time even listening to what was being said. His mind was still mesmerized by the beautiful and timid young lady he had just met. David could hardly wait to get to know and learn more about Hannah.

Lovina sat on the edge of her bed, looking out across the fields of farmland through her bedroom window. Knowing that David was no longer in the house next-door left a hollow emptiness in Lovina's heart. In her eighteen-years, she had never gone a summer without seeing David.

Lovina tired to imagine what her sweet friend was doing at that moment. Did he realize how much she was thinking of him? Did he miss her at all?

Lovina closed her eyes and took a deep breath, "Dear God," she whispered into the darkness, "Please, bring the man that I love back to me."

Chapter Three

David carefully guided his uncle's buggy down the road. It was only his second day in Indiana and work was already starting to pick up; however, Uncle Amos had sent him to town to pick up some nails for a woodworking project he was doing in the barn.

The summer afternoon sun shone down on David and the warmth of the breeze put a smile on his face. David was enjoying his time away from home and, although he had not had many opportunities to spend time with Hannah, he had hopes that would change eventually.

The buggy suddenly took a lung, pulling David out of his thoughts.

"Woah, boy! Woah!" David pulled tightly on the reigns, unsure of what was happening to the buggy. Carefully guiding the horse to the side of the road, he jumped down from his seat and looked over the situation.

Something was wrong with the front buggy wheel. Grabbing a hold of it, David gave it a wiggle, trying to determine if it could keep going.

Pulling off his straw hat, David slapped it against his leg in frustration. He couldn't get to town on that wheel and he didn't think he could make it back to his uncle's house either.

The clipping of oncoming horse hooves made David stand up straighter and wave desperately at the approaching buggy.

The driver was a single Amish man. As soon as David caught his attention, the other driver pulled his buggy to the side of the road behind David.

"Hi there!" David greeted with a smile as he watched the other Amish man get off his buggy and start toward him, "Boy, I sure am glad to see you!" Sticking out a hand, he announced, "I'm David Yoder. I'm staying with my Uncle Amos Yoder – you probably know him."

The stranger nodded and simply said, "I'm Luke Christner." Taking a deep breath, he walked over to the buggy and squatted down to inspect the wheel.

"Looks like this is busted good," he announced, pushing his hat back on his head and reaching up to wipe some sweat from his brow.

David groaned, "I was afraid of that."

Standing to his feet, Luke continued, "I'm afraid you shouldn't drive it any farther than just a few feet or you'll end up wrecking or destroying your entire buggy." With a slight smirk, Luke added, "Lucky for you, this is my parents' drive right up ahead. And I just happen to work on buggies for a living."

David's eyes got large and he let out a huge sigh, "Oh, *gut*! Do you think that you could help me out?"

Luke nodded, "Sure thing. Just lead your buggy down to my workshop. I'll have her fixed up in just a bit."

True to his word, Luke had the buggy wheel fixed within an hour.

David stayed by the young man who had rescued him and worked to fill him in on all the details about his life, his home, and his family. Luke, who seemed to be more reserved, was happy to listen and donate very few details of his own.

"How much do I owe you?" David asked as Luke put the repaired wheel back on his buggy.

Luke gave a shrug as he secured the wheel in place, "Nothing. Consider it a welcome present. Maybe you can help me with one of my horses one day this summer."

"*Ach*," David raised an eyebrow, "I can't let you do that. I took some time you could have been working on other projects..."

Before he could finished, Luke started shaking his head, "No, no you didn't," he assured David as he stood up straight, "Honestly, I didn't have any other work for today." Sighing deeply, he announced, "As badly as we need a horse trainer in this area, we do not need any kind of buggy work. Jobs around here are scarce, David. I was glad to help."

David pondered Luke's statement for a moment. As an idea entered his mind, a broad smile spread across his face, "Listen, Luke! You may not be needed here, but you sure would be in my community! How would you feel about going to Kentucky to spend the summer with my family? It would sure help them out while I'm gone, and you could earn money doing buggy repairs and carpentry work!"

Luke was silent, obviously studying David's suggestion. Finally, with a shrug, he announced, "*Jah* – I don't see why that wouldn't be great. *Danki*, David."

The entire plan made David's face light up like that of a little boy. Grinning from ear-to-ear, he grabbed his new friend's hand in a shake and started making plans to get Luke back to Kentucky.

Chapter Four

Lovina reached up to wipe some sweat from her forehead as she took a break from chopping weeds out of the row of green beans. Despite all her hard work, the weeds were quickly starting to overtake the plants.

David had now been gone two weeks, and Lovina had yet to hear anything from him. His absence made her sad and she wished for all she was worth that she would receive a letter.

Glancing across the field toward his house, she thought of all the times they had snuck away from their chores and played together instead.

To her surprise, Lovina saw a young man approaching her. Could it be...? Lovina's heart dropped as he drew closer. Although she had hoped that it was David, she instantly realized that her eyes had been playing tricks on her. This stranger was even taller than her dear childhood friend and slightly thinner.

"Hullo," Lovina called out as he continued to draw closer.

"Hullo," the stranger returned, his voice deep and almost mysterious, "Are you Lovina Miller?"

Lovina stood up straighter and adjusted her prayer *kapp*, "That would be me. Do I know you?"

The stranger shook his head, "No, you don't." Now he was so close that Lovina was able to get a good look at him. This strange Amish man looked to be in his early twenties, but he seemed more mature. His brown hair was so dark it was almost black, and his eyes a dark color chocolate. Just looking at him made Lovina take a deep breath of surprise. *Ach*, it was hard to remember a time that she had ever seen such a *gut*-looking man!

"I'm Luke Christner. I know your friend, David, and I'm staying with his family until he returns." Glancing toward her house, Luke asked, "Is your *daed* at home? The Yoders told me that he has a construction crew and I'd like a job."

Lovina felt so out of sorts, she wasn't sure what to do. Looking down at her bare feet, she tried to gather her composure. Taking a deep breath, she said, "*Nee*, my *daed* isn't home from work yet, but we're expecting him any minute. If you'd like to wait in the house, my *mamm* can give you some fresh lemonade and cookies."

Luke glanced from the house back to Lovina and then shrugged, "If you don't mind, I'll just stay out here. Looks like you could use some help." Grabbing for an extra hoe, Luke set to work, removing the pesky weeds from among the rows of bean plants.

There was something about Luke that made Lovina feel uncertain about everything. He was a good help in the garden, but she certainly would have felt more at-ease without him. On the other hand, she dreaded him leaving once her father got home from work. Just being near him made her feel things that she had never experienced – she found herself overwhelmed by a sort of giddiness that sprung up from deep within. Although Lovina had always been a talker, she suddenly seemed almost speechless.

"You don't have to do this," Lovina assured him.

Luke simply set his jaw and turned to look at her with his brooding, dark eyes, "I don't have to...but I want to."

Lovina felt weak in the knees, as if she might keel right over. Taking a deep breath, she tried to stead herself.

Suddenly, she found herself a little glad that David was going to be gone for the summer. As quickly as the thought flitted through her mind, she pushed it away; however, just the realization that she could think such a thing left Lovina questioning everything about the future.

David washed his hands in a pail of water that had been set out by the barn, preparing himself for the evening meal. Inside the house, Aunt Miriam was putting the finishing touches on a pot of homemade chili with the help of three of David's cousins.

True to Uncle Amos' word, in the time that David had spent in Indiana he had already been so busy, he hardly had time to even think about being at home.

Wiping his clean hands on a towel, David glanced across the acres of land that his uncle owned. There, in the glowing darkness of the evening, he could make out the form of a young woman walking near the pond.

Hannah.

David had learned to recognize her from a distance. Even though it would be hard to distinguish her from any other Amish woman from so far away, David could pick Hannah out because she was always alone. It seemed like she carried an air of sadness with her, wherever she went.

Taking a deep breath, David stepped out of the barn and started the short walk to the pond.

"Hi there," David called out as he drew near to Hannah.

The young woman looked up at him and gave a sad smile.

"What are you doing?"

Hannah gave a shrug and pulled her black shawl tighter against her shoulders, "I just felt like a walk," she explained.

David stepped up next to her side, "It must be sort of lonely to walk all alone."

Hannah shrugged again, "I'm used to being alone."

David *thought* over his childhood and how little time he had ever spent just to himself. There were always siblings to play with, other Amish children to enjoy at events, and Lovina. Lovina had always been there for him.

Just the thought of his old friend's name sent a nagging sense of guilt through his mind.

Hadn't he promised Lovina that, when he got home, things would be different? Hadn't he promised that they would spend time together? So, what was he doing, trying to get closer to Hannah?

"David…" Hannah's soft voice brought him out of his thoughts, "Are you all right, David? I've never seen you so solemn and quiet."

David looked up at her in surprise, his face breaking out in a broad grin, "Oh, *jah*, I'm fine. I was just thinking is all."

"I didn't know you were able to do that…you know, think without saying what was going through your mind." Although Hannah's words were haughty, David *looked* up in time to catch a teasing smile cross her lips. It was the first time he had ever seen her smile and, something about it made him want to see it a thousand times more.

"Maybe it's too much time around you," David suggested, "Because I don't think you ever say anything much at all."

Hannah's tender smirk turned into a broad smile and David was, once again, captivated by her charm.

Reaching out, he gently took her elbow in his hand, "Would you do me the honor of letting me walk with ya tonight?"

Hannah was silent for a moment, studying David for all that he was worth. Finally, she nodded slowly and said, "*Jah* – I suppose that might be nice."

Chapter Five

Just as David had predicted, it was easy for Luke to find work in Kentucky. He not only spent his afternoons working on buggies in the Yoder's empty shed, but also joined the carpentry work crew lead by Lovina's father.

Lovina wasn't exactly sure how it happened, but it seemed that she and Luke were constantly thrown in the paths of one another. Lovina tried to convince herself that it was merely a coincidence, but she had to admit that it was more than that.

The longer David was gone, the less she was thinking about him and the more she was thinking about Luke.

When he wasn't busy with work, Luke frequently dropped by to help Lovina in the garden; although he wasn't a talker, there was something about his calm attitude that left Lovina yearning for more time with him.

One evening, Lovina baked a plate of her famous homemade ginger snap cookies and decided to take a few across the creek as a thank you for Luke's help in the garden.

Knocking on the shed door, she cautiously pushed it open, cheerfully announcing, "Hello! Luke! Are ya in here?"

"*Jah*, I'm here," Luke replied.

There he was, standing next to a work bench with a busted buggy wheel laid out in front of him.

"Hi there!" Lovina greeted him, suddenly feeling unsure of herself and terribly bashful, "I thought I might bring you something." Placing the plate of cookies on the work table, she watched Luke eyeball them before picking one up and putting it in his mouth.

"It's just a thank you for all the help you've been giving me," she explained.

Luke raised his eyebrows and nodded as he swallowed, "*Danki* – they're very good. You're a good baker, Lovina."

Lovina felt her heart skip a beat with his compliment. Looking at the work he was doing, she added, "Looks like you've got quite a few talents of your own."

Reaching for another cookie, Luke gave a shrug, "I keep busy for sure....but that's a good thing. I'm always thankful for the money."

Leaning back against the table, Lovina studied him in the growing darkness, "Saving back for a farm of your own?"

Luke stared straight at his work and shook his head, "No. I'm going to give my money to help out my family. I have no need of a place of my own."

"Don't you ever hope to get married and have a family?"

Luke shook his head slowly, "I'm afraid all of my dreams are gone. I plan to be alone forever."

His words broke Lovina's heart. Although he tried to sound resolved, it was easy to hear the pain in his voice.

"*Ach*, Luke," she managed to whisper with a smile, "Don't say that. You never know what might happen."

Luke took in a deep breath and then let it out slowly. Looking up to meet Lovina's eyes, he studied her for what seemed minutes before asking, "What about you? Do you think that you could ever love someone like me?"

His question took Lovina by such surprise that she almost fell over. Her eyes growing large, she looked down at the floor, her heart flooded by a million different emotions.

"I...I...Luke..." Lovina's voice was trailing in every direction but her words were making no sense at all.

"Lovina," Reaching out, Luke put his hand on top of hers, "Would you consider going with me to the singing after church this weekend?"

It felt like Lovina would not be able to breath, so many decisions were running helter-skelter through her mind. Almost a surprise to herself, she heard her voice say, "Sure. I don't see why not."

Although David had been staying busy with the horses, he still managed to make some time to help out in the store. With a beautiful girl like Hannah there, he had to find time to spend with her.

One afternoon they had received a large order of supplies and were hurrying to put them on the shelves before it would be too dark to see, even by the glow of the lantern.

"*Ach*, this is a job!" David grumbled as he hurried to put some bags of flour in their place on a shelf, "Of course this would just happen to be the night that Uncle Amos and his entire family went visiting...leaving you and me to do all the work."

Hannah smiled and shook her head, "David, you complain so much. I don't mind the work. Work keeps me busy...work keeps my mind off of...other things."

Suddenly interested, David looked up in surprise. Maybe he would finally have a chance to hear some of the secrets that were hidden away behind this mysterious girl's sad blue eyes.

"What other things?" David asked.

Hannah shrugged as she ran her fingers over a bag of sugar, "Disappointments...heartbreaks...bad decisions."

Hannah went silent, assuring David that he would hear no more of her story, but then she surprised him when she went on to clear her throat and say, "I had a boyfriend...a fiancé even."

As the words came pouring out of her mouth, it was easy to see that they were tearing her apart. Hannah closed her eyes and continued, "But things didn't work out. We were engaged but...well, I was filled with so many uncertainties. I called off the wedding before it was even announced in church. I didn't mean to end everything with him – I just needed more time to think. But I'm afraid he took it as an outright rejection. And now, I'll never have a chance with him again," Hannah reached up to wipe away the tears that were threatening to overwhelm her, "*Ach*, David, it almost breaks my heart to talk about it. I have destroyed all my chances for happiness."

Looking at her in the light of the lantern, her face clouded over with pain and tears gathering in her eyes, David felt totally broken for her. Pulling himself to his feet, he stood up straight and stepped closer to her, putting a hand on her thin shoulder.

"Hannah," he whispered her name with all the tenderness that he had been storing in his heart, "Dear Hannah...you still have a thousand chances for happiness." Reaching up, he took his thumb and brushed a tear off of her cheek.

Hannah took a deep breath and let it out slowly. Looking at him in surprise, she simply whispered, "*Danki*, David." Then she squared her shoulders and announced, "Let's get back to work."

Chapter Six

Over the next few days, David and Hannah had little time to spend together. He looked forward to ever chance he had to see her. Although their friendship had not had time to progress, David felt confident that over the rest of the summer he could easily earn himself a special place in Hannah's lonely heart.

One afternoon, David had finally found a chance to work in the dry goods store alongside Hannah when one of his cousins came rushing into the shed with a letter in his outstretched hand.

"David," the little cousin called out, "You got some mail!"

Taking the letter, David quickly recognized the handwriting as that of his younger sister, Lydia.

Ripping the seal open, David pulled out the letter, unsure why his teenage sister would even take the time to write him.

Dear David,

I don't want to bother you while you're gone, but I need to let you know something important. I've always thought that you and Lovina had something special together, although I'm not sure if you had any kind of plans for the future or an agreement. While you've been gone, Lovina has taken a spark to the very man you sent here to work – Luke Christner. Seems like they're seeing each other almost every day and last night I overheard him invite her to the singing Sunday night. She agreed to go with him.

I don't mean to stick my nose in where it doesn't belong, but I know that you were always sweet on Lovina and just thought you should know.

Your sister,

Lydia

"*Ach*," David read over the letter and then reread it again, his heart suddenly dropping into his stomach.

Lovina – with Luke? A multitude of emotions suddenly assailed David. He found himself so frustrated, almost angry at Luke for stealing his girl. How dare Luke go to David's own home and try to take the woman he loved away from him? David was hurt, so hurt, by Lovina's decision to move forward with a relationship with someone else. But, worst of all, David felt incredible guilt and sadness.

Deep in his heart, David realized that it was his own fault that Lovina and Luke were growing close. In all the time that David had been in Indiana, he had never taken the time to even write his childhood sweetheart a letter – he had just always taken for granted that she would be there for him when he returned.

While he had been busy pursing a friendship with Hannah, he had never thought that Lovina might be looking at someone else.

Reaching up, David rubbed his hand across his face, trying to gather his wits and decide what to do next.

"What is wrong, David?" Hannah asked softly as she stepped up next to him.

David balled his free hand up into a fist, fighting the urge to destroy the letter he had just received. Passing it to Hannah, he quickly explained, "I don't know how to tell you this, Hannah, but Lovina...well, she and I have always been friends. I don't mean to have led you astray in any way because I have liked you since the day we met but this..." David couldn't go on.

Hannah took the letter in her own hands and read it slowly, her eyes growing large as she went over the message again and again.

"David," she managed to breath softly, "What are you going to do?"

David brushed his hand through his hair as memories of Lovina ran across his mind, "I don't know. I just don't know." Turning, he gave the floor a hard kick with the toe of his boot.

"David," Hannah took a deep breath and shook her head slowly, "I hate to say this, but you know that we aren't meant to be together. No matter how happy we might have both been to pretend...it just isn't so. You have made my summer much more enjoyable...but it's time to get back to our real lives."

David looked down at his feet. He wanted to fight her words; he hated the idea of giving Hannah up completely. But, when he thought of his dear Lovina...he knew that he couldn't live without her.

"Go to her, David!" Hannah exclaimed, "Go to Lovina and let her know that you love her."

Taking a deep breath, David nodded his head, "I'll go call a driver right now."

Chapter Seven

David sat in the passenger seat of the truck, half-heartedly listening as his driver talked incessantly during the long trip back home. Looking out the window, David watched the scenery slowly change from the flat Amish country of Indiana to the rolling hills of Kentucky.

With each mile that passed, it seemed that David got even more nervous about his future with Lovina.

When he first started home, he had been certain that she would be glad to see him but now...well, the closer he got to her, the less sure he became. Maybe she had truly fallen for Luke and she wouldn't want to even see him. Maybe David had blown his one and only chance for true love with the only girl he ever truly cared for.

Lovina had just filled up a bucket of water and got down on her knees to scrub the kitchen floor with a scrub brush when she heard a truck pull up in the front yard.

Ach, Lovina thought to herself as she plunged her hands down into the soapy water, *Daed must have visitors.*

It was Saturday afternoon and Lovina found her mind plagued with thoughts of Luke and their upcoming date. Although she truly enjoyed spending time with him, there was something about agreeing to go on a date with him that put her mind entirely in a tizzy. As much as she liked Luke and was attracted to him, Lovina battled thoughts of David – it seemed so sad to be turning her back on their relationship with each other.

But, she reasoned to herself, when she thought back on it, she and David had never had a true relationship. Sure, he had always been a good friend to her, but it seemed that was all things were to ever be. Since he left for Indiana, she had not heard a word from him and, as sad as she was to admit it, she was starting to wonder if he would ever come home at all.

"Lovina."

The voice seemed to come out of no where. Lovina looked up in surprise, wondering if she was truly hearing a person or if it was her own imagination.

There, standing in the doorway to the kitchen, was David himself.

"David!" Lovina managed to breathe as she struggled to pull herself to her feet, "Oh, David...is that really you?"

In an instant, David had bridged the space between them. He came right to her side, nearly knocking her bucket of soapy water over in his hurry.

"Lovina," David managed to say, somewhat louder this time, "Lovina…" he seemed to want to say more, but acted as if he couldn't find the words. Reaching out, he grabbed Lovina and gathered her into his arms.

To Lovina, everything felt like a crazy dream. Pressed firmly against her old friend's body, all thoughts of Luke vanished from her mind as she let David hold her like a little girl.

"Lovina," David pulled back only long enough to kiss her on the mouth, "Lovina, I have been a total moron. I am so sorry!"

"David," Lovina managed to say as she tried to catch her breath, "David…what has happened?"

David stepped back as he struggled to gather his composure. Reaching up, he wiped away at tears that threatened to overtake him.

"Lovina," he reached out and held her hands in his own, "I have been so ignorant. I left home, anxious to find adventure and experience new things…and I almost lost the one thing that means the most to me in the world – you."

Lovina felt her heart start to melt as David poured out his soul to her, "Lovina, I love you. I love you more than I ever realized. I thought that Uncle Amos was giving me a chance to experience adventure but I think it was actually the good Lord allowing me the opportunity to realize how much I love you. Please, Lovina…I don't want to wait any longer. Say that you will marry me!"

There had never been anything that Lovina wanted more. In that instant, it felt like all of her hopes and dreams were finally coming true.

Luke.

The name entered her mind suddenly and it felt like the life was drained right out of her. Oh, but hadn't she already led him to believe that she cared for him? Hadn't she already agreed to go out on a date with him this very weekend?

"David," Lovina squeezed her dear friend's hands tightly as she looked for the right words to share her news, "David. I have been a foolish girl."

"And I have been a foolish man," David was quick to add.

Lovina smiled and shook her head, "Perhaps we've both been foolish…"

Her words were cut short as the sound of an approaching vehicle brought them both from their thoughts.

Glancing out the window, they watched together as a strange car stopped in front of the house and let out a passenger.

David felt his heart sink when he saw the visitor who was getting out of the strange car.

It was Hannah.

David thought that she had understood. What was she doing…following him all the way to Kentucky of all places? Hadn't she been the one who had said that their relationship wasn't going to work and even pushed him to return to Lovina? What was she doing here now?

David battled the urge to run forward and stop her before she could get to the house. Turning to Lovina, he struggled to find the words to explain what was surely about to come.

"Lovina…" he hurried to say, "While I was gone, I was an idiot. I hate telling you this more than you will ever know, but I got involved with a girl from Indiana. We never started to court, but we were heading in that direction when I heard that you and Luke had begun a relationship…."

As the words poured from his mouth, David watched Lovina's face turn ashen and then red with shame.

"You already know about Luke?" She managed to whisper.

David nodded his head, "That was the wake-up call I needed. That was what I needed to bring me back home. I never want to risk losing you again, Lovina!"

Lovina started to wipe tears away from her eyes, "David, I don't want to lose you either! But what you heard is true. Luke and I have grown close and are on the verge of starting a relationship. I was so foolish, David, but I was afraid I had lost you and now I don't know what to do..."

In the other room, they could hear a knock on the front door.

Wiping at her eyes, Lovina hurried to go open it with David trailing close behind. When she opened the door, Hannah was standing on the front porch, a determined look in her blue eyes.

"I need to talk to David," she announced, looking from Lovina to David.

"David," she took a deep breath, "I need to go to your house...I need to see Luke."

Luke? David was more confused than ever. Cocking his head to one side, he tried to understand where this strange twist came into play.

"You don't have to look far," the deep voice of Luke spoke out and they all turned in surprise to find that he had come up on the porch and was standing just out of view.

"Hannah," as he said the name, his voice seemed to fill with a strange sort of pain.

"*Ach*, Luke..." Hannah looked down at her black shoes as if she couldn't hold his gaze, "I have been wanting to talk to you."

Luke shook his head sadly, "I can't imagine what we would have to say to each other now."

"Luke...you know that I am a very shy girl," Hannah said in a shaky voice, "And I have let my fear get the better of me far too many times. I almost let it destroy what we had together. But Luke...I can't let that happen."

David's eyes got large as he realized that Luke must be the ex-beau that Hannah had told him about.

"I love you, Luke," Hannah announced resolutely, "I love you and I still want to be your wife...if you can ever find it in your heart to have me."

David watched Luke and held his breath, hoping that he would agree.

Stepping forward, Luke reached out and took Hannah in his arms, "I love you too, Hannah!" He exclaimed as he cupped her face in his hands, "I have always loved you and I always will." Turning to look at Lovina, he quickly tried to explain, "Lovina, I hope that you understand..."

Lovina smiled broadly as she wrapped her arms around David's waist, "It is fine, Luke. I think that things are exactly the way that they are supposed to be!"

Epilogue

Standing together at the kitchen sink, Lovina and David watched as a group of children played outside in their front yard.

"Look at those crazy things," Lovina muttered as she noticed her daughter trying to climb a tree.

"Just like us when we were little," David announced.

Lovina looked up at him and smirked, "*Jah* – and I think our little girl might have a crush on the neighbor boy, as well."

David and Lovina had now been married for ten years and had three children of their own. It had been a double wedding shared with Hannah and Luke, who decided to move to Kentucky so that Luke would continue to enjoy a steady stream of work.

David and Lovina had built their house behind his parents' place and, to their surprise, Hannah and Luke had bought a piece of farm land right across the creek.

Their children played together and it wouldn't be any surprise if someday those same children would grow up to marry one another.

David smiled broadly and gathered his wife up in his arms.

"I'm glad I went to Indiana that summer," he announced as he reached out to push a strand of her brown hair back from her face, "Because that summer showed me how much I need you in my life."

Bending over, he gave her a gentle kiss.

Life truly was as David and Lovina had always imagined it – and they were happier than they ever could have guessed possible.

THE END